COMING OUT

tom

sylvia aguilar-zéleny

EPIC
Press

Tom
Coming Out: Book #1

Written by Sylvia Aguilar-Zéleny

Copyright © 2016 by Abdo Consulting Group, Inc.

Published by EPIC Press™
PO Box 398166
Minneapolis, MN 55439

Printed in the United States of America.

Cover design by Nicole Ramsay
Images for cover art obtained from Shutterstock.com
Edited by Nancy Cortelyou

LIBRARY OF CONGRESS CATALOGING-IN-PUBLICATION DATA

Aguilar-Zéleny, Sylvia.
Tom / Sylvia Aguilar-Zéleny.
p. cm. — (Coming out)
Summary: Tom's secret relationship with Sean, the most popular guy in school,
saves him from the cruelty of his mother, and the indifference of his father.
But when everything falls apart, Tom must face his inner demons alone.
ISBN 978-1-68076-012-5 (hardcover)
1. Homosexuality—Fiction. 2. Gays—Fiction. 3. Gay teenagers—Fiction.
4. Coming out (Sexual orientation)—Fiction. 5. Young adult fiction. I. Title.
[Fic]—dc23
2015932734

To the memory of Blake Brockington, and everyone who struggles to be who they are

CHAPTER ONE
an insect

THIS IS HOW I REMEMBER IT.

At some point I open my eyes and see the shower-head and basket of shampoo above me. I try closing my eyes again but can't. I spring up. I am startled. It takes me a second to realize the where and how of the mess I am in. The where is easy: in a bathtub full of water. The how: that's a lot more complicated. I took a bunch of my pills. I tried to kill myself and failed.

Fuck. I decide to put my fingers down my throat and puke it all out. I feel dizzy. I feel sick. But I am alive.

This isn't my first failure. I've actually failed at everything important in my life so far.

I sucked big time at playing with cars and action figures as a kid. I never liked baseball, basketball, or football, and, of course, I didn't make it onto any team, which led to me failing my family. I also failed at all the sports and outdoors activities that Dad and Uncle Robert would take my brother and me to. I failed my mom in piano. Dancing was more my thing, but mom said that was for fags.

"What's a fag?" I asked when I was five or six years old. I got no answer. Years later, after the Charlie Dale Incident at St. Mary's Catholic School, the word FAG was written on my locker, but by then I already knew what the word meant. It had never occurred to me, though, that that's who or what I was—a fag.

My life is a long list of shitty misfortunes. Not being able to fix things with Sean is only the most recent.

As I try to get out of my own mess, I realize my stupid parents are already home. I can hear my mother's craziness in the kitchen. She's fixing dinner while listening to the news—that's her thing, you know. The sounds of pots, pans, and silverware are always interrupted by her saying, "fucking shit," or "goddamnit," every time she messes up or something on TV makes her angry. It is almost seven p.m. so Dad has probably already crawled into his studio and is now focusing all his attention on the latest issue of *Insects' World* magazine or any of his books about insects in Peru, Taiwan, or wherever.

The bathroom is a sauna. I can't even see myself in the mirror. Not like I want to though. I touch my lower lip: pain, pain, pain. For a split second I think of going downstairs and just telling them what happened, but what is the point? I know the drill. Mom will say, "What the fuck were you thinking?" or the classic, "Why are you doing this to me?"

Dad. Dad will just stare, not say a word, and will crawl back to his studio, like the insect he is. Dad hides from the human world. He wasn't always like that though. I remember a time when he would invent stories for us before we went to bed. Anyway, he doesn't do that anymore. He's always quiet now. And nowadays my family dynamics go like this: Mom yells and Dad just closes his door. The End.

Dad is more like a closet Dad, you know? He doesn't want to come out as an actual Dad. In my family, Mom calls the shots. Dad is just a pussy. I thought, *I better not say anything or she'll send me straight to the teen mental clinic. Again.* The clinic might as well be my second home.

I have always hated this feeling. The pruning up, that disgusting feeling on my skin. It's stupid; as a swimmer, I always get pruned up. This time is different: the pruning up feels like it's inside me too.

"A prune, I am a prune," I tell myself. "A fucking failing prune who should just go to his room and check his phone." I wonder if Sean texted back.

I flush the toilet and as I open the bathroom door my mom yells, "Thomas? You home already?"

I want to say, "Yes, it's me, Mom. I just took a couple million more of the fucking pills the doctor prescribed so I can be a good boy. Oh yeah, and I

tried to sink myself in the tub but it didn't work."
Instead, I simply say, "Got out of practice early."

* * *

Once in my room I check my phone. No text messages.
The words I have written to him so far look so
lonely on my screen. Like one of those monologues
Mr. Reuben, my English professor, makes us read
in class.

Maybe he hasn't unfriended me on Facebook? I
should just send him an email or call him, yes, call
him . . .

I call him. No answer. *Yeah, why would he?* I tell
myself.

"Thomas, dinner is almost ready!" Mom yells.

I know there's no way they would notice anything odd about me, I mean, not more than they
have noticed my whole life. You see, for my parents,
I am not only a failure, but also a weirdo. When
Mom talks to me, she doesn't even look me in the

eyes, like I make her uncomfortable or something. Dad looks at me, or does he? Maybe I'm the one who doesn't look at him. Maybe we haven't looked at each other in years.

I decide to text Sean one more time:

Sean. Please, we need to talk.

I really fucked it up.

But Sean hasn't unfriended me; I can still see his shit. I can read what he and God think about us fags and the two hundred and ten "likes" his posts got.

"You weren't so picky about *this* fag who sucked your brains out just the other day, were you?" I tell him, or rather, I tell his Facebook profile picture.

I want to write something on my Facebook wall, something witty, something that would shut everyone up. But what can I write? The whole thing felt like those times when Mom and I would argue and I wouldn't know what to say to her until hours or days later. The best words escape you when you need them the most. It is funny though that Sean posted something at all—he doesn't like Facebook all that much. It's like he's using it just to upset me. His girlfriend seems to like the whole thing a lot.

She posted: My boyfriend has a gay stalker. That says a lot about my good taste in men, right?

Stupid Hanna. To think I kinda felt pity for her. Just imagine being the official girlfriend of the swim team's star and said star preferred to make out now and then with the second best swimmer of the team. That's me, by the way. That does say a lot about her "good" taste in men, right? Maybe that's what I should post:

Forgive me for my taste in men!

Fucking bitch. I hate her now.

* * *

I don't want to come down to dinner, but Mom keeps calling me.

"Thomas, goddamnit, it's the third time I've called you. Dinner is getting cold."

I sit down across from Dad and he smiles at me,

until he sees it. *It.* "What's that?" Dad points at my bloody lip.

"Are you okay? Did you get in a fight?" he adds.

"It's nothing."

"Do you . . . You know, do you want to . . . tell us about it?"

Dad and his pauses when he doesn't want to talk.

My way to say, "No, I don't want to fucking talk about it," is to stay quiet. My silence takes him back to his salad. Mom then says, "Please don't tell me you got yourself in trouble again, Thomas, because . . . "

Mom and her threats for anything that she might find threatening for herself. I say, "It's nothing. An accident. That's all." My lip is slightly bleeding. I can taste my own blood.

"Clean yourself up," she says, passing me a napkin before changing the subject.

"I called Jeremy today. He didn't answer, so I left him a message. Have you talked to him?" Mom asks Dad.

"Talked to who?" asks Dad.

"Jeremy, your son, remember? The one you sent to Montreal."

"Oh."

Long, long, long pause.

"So have you talked to him lately?" Mom asks Dad.

"No."

Conversation over.

They do not say anything else about my lip. I finish eating, then pick up my plate and excuse myself before going back to my room.

Maybe Sean has texted by now. Maybe he thought things over, I tell myself. Maybe he apologized. Maybe he says that I did fuck things up, but we can continue cautiously, in secret.

Nope.

My phone's screen continues to be a long monologue. I add, Sean, I'm sorry. I know I really fucked up this time.

It's just Wednesday, so I still have some days of school to face it all. *Fuck, there's practice tomorrow afternoon*, I remind myself. I'm sure the whole team will give me one of those *we-know-it-all* or *we-almost-know-it-all* kinda looks. You know: my version of the story and what Sean had introduced as the original version of the story. In his version, I'm the evil gay dude, the pervert who tried to take advantage of the naïve star of the swim team.

I must stop calling him the *star*. He doesn't even deserve it. He's a fake. Phony. He is . . . He is . . .

Just like me.

CHAPTER TWO
meeting sean

THIS IS MY FIRST MEMORY OF IT.

Mom was fixing Dad's tie for Sunday Mass and said, "When you guys grow up, you will wear a tie just like your dad."

My brother Jeremy, who was ten years old at the time, said, "Yes, a tie and a jacket."

I was only six and already felt like, *A tie? Me?* All I really wanted was that beautiful funky necklace she wore everywhere. I looked at her and like a dumbass, I said, "I wanna wear your necklace."

She got pissed and said, "Don't be stupid."

Later that day Jeremy told me, "Boys don't wear necklaces, you moron."

She knew—she had to have known. She knew her son was a fag. A failure.

If she didn't know it then, she knew it when she asked me what I wanted to be when I grew up and I happily answered, "A ballerina." She was mad, and I was sent to the basement for hours with no food. "I'm not hungry anyway," I yelled at her before she slammed the door.

She knew it. She knew about me when my choir teacher told her I was holding hands with that other kid—what was his name? Mom yanked my arm so hard that it hurt for a week and no more choir class for me. Or those couple of times she found me playing fashion runway wearing a ton of her accessories.

So, she knows. And she has always tried to beat the gay out of me every fucking time something or someone reminded her of it. She still does. You gotta give it to her, her ways get more creative with time. Just the other day she gave away my red skinny jeans. "Too gay," that's all she said. I told her to fuck off and that only got me a big soap-opera slap. Just so you know, slaps are my mom's signature.

1. You talk back, slap.
2. You lie, slap.
3. You tell her to fuck off, slap.
4. You wear her makeup, slap.
5. Slap.
6. Slap.
7. Slap.

The thing is, her son—her youngest son—is gay, and the only way she can deal with it is by making me her punching bag. My body has become a map of her rage, and mine as well. Sometimes I don't know which scars are hers and which are mine. Cause I have done some work on my own. Scar over scar.

I'm a failure, and not because I am a fag; although, given how fucked up things are right now, it seems like I've failed as a fag too. No, I'm a failure in general. I see myself like one of those insects Dad has read about all his life, one worth squishing.

"Some insects get to kill themselves. For different reasons, of course," thoughtful Dad said the last time I screwed things up.

And I was thinking, *I don't even get to be one of those interesting insects.*

The truth is, part of me liked it when Dad told me insect stories, but part of me hated those insects. I hated how he gave more attention to them.

When I was in elementary school, Dad used to have an ant farm. He spent hours and hours with it, whole weekends just looking at them. I hated them. One day Jeremy and I were bored to death because Mom had taken the TV from us or had forbidden us to go and play outside—anyway, I told Jeremy, "Let's kill them. Let's kill Dad's ants." He didn't want to.

He kept saying Dad would be mad. "He loves the ants more than anything in the world," he said.

"Exactly. More than us. We gotta teach him a lesson."

Jeremy kept saying, "No, no, no."

I looked at him and said, "You are such a pussy."

So I did it on my own. I poured soda and salt and detergent on them all. It was crazy. Jeremy tried to stop me. "I'm gonna tell Dad," he kept saying. But I knew he wouldn't dare. Then we heard the door, "It's Mom, Tom! Mom! She's gonna kill us!" She didn't, though, she just yelled at us for the mess. Maybe Mom also hated having those ants at home.

Dad just asked us, "Why did you do it?" Jeremy started crying, and kept saying, "Sorry, Dad. Sorry."

I went, "It was my idea. I did it because they weren't so interesting to me."

He patted my shoulder and said, "I really loved my ants. I wish you hadn't done this to them."

Sometime after that incident, Dad created a new farm. He kept it at his office this time, away from us—I mean, away from me. No more insects at home, except for me. I became the insect.

I never got into his studio except of course for those times that I had to knock on his door to tell him, "Dinner is ready," or "Mom needs you," or

"There's someone at the door looking for you." It's like we made a deal without making a deal, a deal of not entering into each other's world. Yes, Dad also stopped coming into my room. He sorta walked out of my life.

Jeremy walked out too. Never again did we play in his room. Never again did we play together. Something broke between us. Something that none of us tried to fix. He became the kid who happened to be my brother.

After the ant incident, he asked Mom for a room of his own. Mom happily destroyed our playroom to make it Jeremy's. Childhood was over that day. Childhood or brotherhood, maybe both.

"I hate my brother," I told everyone. The few conversations between Jeremy and me became pretty much like our parents': monosyllables. "Yes." "No." "Maybe."

I hate to admit that I missed him at first. We did have good times when we were kids, Jeremy and me. He cared. He actually cared for me. Why? I don't know. Really, I look back at all of those many times when he had to put up with my doing ballet in the middle of our room or my wearing Mom's clothes. Jeremy just let me be. He would just say, "Mom is coming, you better change. If she sees you wearing *that*, she'll kill you."

I don't think Jeremy understood why I did what I did or who I was. I mean he too was a kid. He was only four years older than me, but I'm sure it was clear to him that his little brother was a mess. I wonder why it was no big deal for him.

He never once questioned me for doing it. It's not like I always did it. You see, I wasn't queer all the time. Dressing up was just something I liked doing once in a while. Mostly I liked playing with Legos and reading books or comics.

Jeremy was very different. He was everything I wasn't. Jeremy is everything I'm not. My brother was fearless and an inveterate jock. Back then I was cautious and not into sports. He was always trying to get me to be like him, more outgoing.

I remember those times he would push me to go and play outside with the rest of the kids on our block, and I would say no, no, no because my favorite show was on TV or because I was *just* about to finish *this* book. Sometimes it was true, but sometimes it was a lie and Jeremy knew it.

He once told me half-jokingly, "You are afraid by being afraid." Who knows what he meant exactly. Jeremy is like Dad, almost never opens his mouth, but when he does, well, something big comes out.

Anyway, even though Jeremy and I "broke up," he still didn't want me to be in trouble. He still took care of me, of us. Of course, I'm sure it was only because if I got myself in trouble, he got in trouble, too. If a glass or a plate was broken or dirty or gone, it was always our fault—not mine, not his, ours.

So much for brotherhood.

* * *

Dr. Stevens would ask, "Did you really want to end your life?"

I wouldn't know what to say. Do I? Do I really want to die? No. Not really, it's just that I felt like dying in that moment. I still do. No one would understand this. Well, maybe Dr. Stevens would. He's the only one who understands me. His saying is, "If someone wants to really commit suicide, he or she does it and that's it. The rest, those who fail, are looking for something else."

Then, of course he would add, "So, Tom, what is this about?"

I felt stupid when I finally started opening up to him, but at the same time I was able to see that what I felt was actually a *thing*, a valid thing.

I should've called Dr. Stevens before I did what I did, before I tried to overdose with my own pills. He would have saved me from my stupidity like he did before.

It was my last year of middle school at St. Mary's. Charlie Dale and I had been best friends since forever. We were both the youngest in the family. He had an older sister; I had an older brother. We both liked the same kinds of books, we both sucked at PE, our mothers knew each other, and we felt comfortable with each other. Charlie was my first best friend. I don't know if at some point between elementary and middle school I felt attracted to Charlie or not. I didn't think of him that way then, I just knew that I loved him.

Anyway, Charlie and I were always together, and when his grandma died I fucking wrote the cheesiest letter telling him how much I understood him. My grandma hadn't died yet, but we stopped seeing her because of my stupid mother. I explained to him how in moments like this, one feels lost or unloved. I told him not to worry because he had my love. Long story short, everybody read or heard about it and I became a joke. "Thomas loves Charlie. Thomas loves Charlie," was said or written all over school. I never found out how everybody read my letter. It didn't matter. What mattered is that I became the joke of the school.

Then came the Ball Incident. Remember that scene in *Carrie*? Now picture me instead of her under a shower of shame—at least it wasn't blood. St. Mary's dance parties were a big deal, both for the school and for the students. It was the day you got to dress up however you wanted. It was when you were allowed to actually have fun in school. We were allowed to laugh out loud, to be ourselves. I had considered not going, but stupid me decided to go.

Everyone had someone to talk to, someone to dance with. Everyone but me. Then I noticed that Charlie was on his own, too, or so I thought. I walked towards him. "Hey, Charlie," I yelled. He didn't hear me. I tried again, only louder. Our classmates heard me, and it all started: the mocking, the bullying—

"Leave Charlie alone."

"Stop stalking him,"

"Go away, FAG."

I can still hear voices yelling FAG, FAG, FAG! Everyone yelling as if I were a leper being chased out of town.

I found in myself a courage I didn't know I had and I told everyone to fuck off. But I felt like shit. I cried my way home and I just wanted to die, but how? I remember seeing pills in Mom's medicine cabinet, so as soon as I got home, I went straight to Mom's room, emptied her cabinet, and cried my soul out as I took one pill after another and blacked out.

My life would soon be over.

Next thing doctors and nurses were pumping my stomach. That's all I remember. Just thinking about it makes me want to puke. My parents did what all loving parents do: sent their son to a clinic. At least it wasn't one of those places where they try to kick the gay out of you.

Dr. Stevens was my third or fourth doctor, I think. I was such a pain in the ass to everyone—no therapist, social worker, doctor or nurse could stand me. I would try to manipulate everyone around me. I was fucking difficult. I told everyone to fuck off. I told everyone that I wanted to go home, that I wasn't going to be cured with their stupid methods, that was until Dr. Stevens came along and set me straight, figuratively speaking. He was the one who helped me understand myself.

So while back home everyone enjoyed the end of the school year and graduation and summer and pools and picnics and the freedom of not having to go to school, I was in a mental clinic learning to survive my self-destructive soul. I was sent there to figure out what was wrong with me.

It took me a while to find that out—find out who I was. It took me scars, tears, and a long list of doctors. Dr. Stevens opened a door to me, he taught me to love who I was.

By the time I left the teen mental clinic, paperwork had already been submitted to transfer me to a public school.

"Riverside High School will suit you better. Besides, it has one of the best swim teams," Mom said. "That will distract you."

"Distract me from what?"

"From whatever goes on in your mind."

"But . . . What about my friends?"

"Who, the librarian? Or are you still friends with Charlie?"

Mom is like a Cruella de Vil of modern times. She would dress in kids' skins if she could.

But I officially ended my private-school education and became a student at Riverside High. And to everyone's surprise—even my own—I liked it. At Riverside, no one knew anything about me. I was a world to discover and there were people who wanted to. Like Lyla for starters: She was the school's gossip machine, and also some sort of welcoming committee. She and I became friends easily, all because we were both wearing *Blondie* t-shirts. What are the chances? She asked me if I had really heard of that band. I said, "I'm Debbie Harry's bastard son." We both laughed. Lyla and I shared a taste for fashion from the 70s and 80s.

I introduced myself to Ron and Mary. One, because they were in most of my classes; and two, because they smart-assed both students and teachers. Ron is a fucking mathematic genius. I'm sure he will grow up to receive a Nobel Prize for science. Mary will be the next great thinker of all times—she's a fucking literary encyclopedia in jeans. But they are not the typical nerds that everyone avoids in school. They are the nerds that everyone fears in school.

Ron and Mary like each other but they don't seem to realize it: they are both morons when it comes to human contact. Watching them interact and blush and flirt without flirting is my favorite sport. I considered helping them see their feelings for each other, but Lyla is right—it's too much fun to see them lost like that. "They are like a daily romantic comedy to watch, dude. Don't turn it off," Lyla told me once.

Lyla, Mary, and Ron became my gang. We were

all freshmen trying to figure out a way to survive the sophomores. So everything started going well in my new school, but the best was still to come: meeting Sean.

* * *

I made it onto the swim team and it was there at the pool where I met my future first boyfriend, Sean.

Boyfriend, is that what he was? What do you call the guy you see, text, call, and hang out with every single day? What do you call the guy you make out with when no one is around? What do you call the guy you have sex with for the first time? What do you call the guy who tells you he loves you and wishes things were easier but does not dare to step out of the closet?

Boyfriend, right?

Well, there you go. Sean was my boyfriend, although everyone around us thought we were just good friends, even my friends and my parents. Mom never actually met him, she just heard me saying, "I'm going out with Sean, be back later." Dad knew Sean. He actually knew everyone on the swim team. He used to hang out with us at the pool. He sat on the bleachers and watched our practices and tried not to miss a single one of our competitions even if it was out of town. I was not all that crazy about him being around *my* practice, but he seemed to like it. To tell you the truth, I liked the faces he made when I beat my personal records.

Sean liked Dad, he really did. Sean used to defend him. He would say that it wasn't only that Dad didn't know how to be a dad, but that I also didn't know how to approach him as a son. Who knows, maybe Sean was right.

* * *

You are probably wondering what happened between me and Sean and how it is that I ended up trying

31

to kill myself. Easy. Even though I had promised Sean I would keep our relationship a secret, I ended up talking about it with Lyla. Yes, I told Lyla, even though she and I had not hung out together all that much since I met Sean. So why, why did I tell Lyla about us? That's the million dollar question. You might be thinking that the reasonable thing to do was to just open up to Ron or Mary, who were more cautious. Did I forget to mention that Lyla is a walking gossip monster? Forget Facebook, Lyla is the best way to spread news. So, why her? I can keep saying that I just couldn't keep it a secret. I can say that what happened between Sean and me during that weekend was so fucking awesome that I had to share it, but I would be lying. It's not that I couldn't keep it a secret. I *didn't want* to keep it a secret. I wanted to tell. I wanted people to know. I *wanted*—yes, I fucking did.

Was this an act of self-sabotage or plain stupidity? Be my judge.

Basically, Sean and I had been seeing each other

for a while and it was like a whole big secret and shit, but once we had sex, instead of keeping it to myself or writing it in a fucking Dear Diary I went and told Lyla, and Lyla told Hanna, and before you know it, Sean heard about it.

And that's how it all started.

I was walking to school and suddenly Sean's car was next to me.

"Get in!"

"What's up?"

"Just get in, we need to talk."

"But I have chemistry and . . . "

"Get-in-the-car."

So I got in the car. He drove out of the student's parking lot and up to Dale Avenue. He was speeding.

"Dude, slow down!"

"Shut up!"

It really wasn't like him to be yelling at the top of his lungs. Actually, that was the first time I heard him screaming at all, he was mad. So mad.

"What's going on?"

But I knew, I fucking knew what was going on. I felt my face burning. My words about us had gotten to him. I was in deep shit.

It started to rain as we were driving to Scenic Road. Our place. The car was quickly covered with raindrops. Inside the glass was all steamy. I reached and tried to clean it for him.

"Fuck, Tom, you are just messing it up, quit it!"

"I'm sorry. I . . . " I wasn't talking about the glass but it didn't matter.

"Can't you just shut up?" You see, Sean never yells. Sean had never asked me to shut up. Sean had never talked to me like that. He was not himself, he sounded more like . . . like me.

He was pissed.

I, Thomas Fischer, had been able to make Sean Donovan mad. Sean, the school's sweetest guy, the *I-can-help-you-with-that* kinda guy. The one who would spend a day helping old people cross the street or rescuing cats stuck on roofs or in trees. He was fucking pissed off and I was to blame.

At some point, Sean stopped speeding, but everything still seemed to be moving fast: houses, sidewalks, parks, stop signs, him, me. Us. Everything. He was squeezing the steering wheel as if that's what he wanted to do to me.

Then, he parked. Turned off the car, released the steering wheel, and said with a tone that was like a cocktail of anger and sadness, "Why did you open your mouth to . . . ? Why? Why did you talk to her? Hanna knows, everybody knows. You destroyed it all, Tom—all. If my parents find out . . . "

"Well, just tell everybody I lied."

"I did. I will. It's just—you don't get it, do you?" He started crying.

I should have said I was sorry. I should have begged him to forgive me. I should have promised to say I was lying. Should have gotten us out of this—what am I saying?—gotten HIM out of this. Isn't that what one is supposed to do for the person they love? I should have done *anything* but open my mouth and let a shitload of my bullshit out.

"Well, I didn't know I wasn't supposed to talk about *my* life to anyone."

"This is *my* life you decided to talk about, Tom. Understand that? We had an agreement."

"Well, I didn't sign any paper, and it isn't *me* who has decided to live inside a closet after all."

There. Sean raised his head, cleaned his tears, and opened my door.

"Get-the-hell-out-of-my-car."

That's when I should have got out and walked back to school.

But I didn't.

"Now you want me out of your car? Have you forgotten that you started everything precisely in this car?"

Sean lost it. I can't blame him.

He started pushing me around, shoulders, arms. Crying, crying, crying. He pushed me out of his car. I should have made him stop. I should have said I was sorry. Instead, I let him do it.

When he was finally able to get me out of the car, he got out of it himself and as I was lying on the sidewalk, he pulled me up by my shirt and hit me. His right fist landed on my face. One time. "Why Tom, why?" Two times. Before he tried again, I yelled, "BECAUSE I WANTED TO, OKAY? I told about us because I WANTED TO. There, I said it."

Sean got into his car, threw my backpack out the window, and left me there.

I did the only thing you can do in those cases. Stand up, clean up, and walk back to school in the rain. The whole way I repeated to myself, "How could you be such an asshole, Tom?"

* * *

I think that meeting Sean was the best thing that could have happened to me. It was also the worst thing. A few months ago, Mom and Dad were fighting. Wait, no, Mom was yelling, Dad was spacing out. You know, a very *Meet The Fischer's* moment. When she was done, she left. Dad was on his way to his studio when I asked him, "Why do you let her talk to you like that?"

Dad didn't look upset or embarrassed or anything.

"Love brings out the best and the worst in you. One day you will understand," he said.

Then, like the insect he is, he crawled silently to his studio and closed the door. I was like, "What the fuck?" But my dad has always been like that. He's quiet, so quiet, and suddenly he says something big as hell then he goes back to being quiet.

Now I understand it, love does bring out the best and worst in you.

I made Sean a better swimmer and Sean made me a better swimmer. He made me less of an asshole and now he's turned me back to my normal assholy state. Sean has also shown his worst side.

Not only did he push me out of his car and punch me but he made quite a scene in the cafeteria later that day.

First, I was a bit late for lunch because I was fucking cleaning myself up after the scene with Sean. So when I got to the cafeteria I could not find Mary or Ron, much less Lyla, and either every seat in every table was taken or the looks on everyone's faces seemed to be saying, "Don't you dare sit here." What was left but sitting in the only available table, the one right next to the garbage cans?

I was there eating on my own when Sean came along. His face showed me right away he was there to start a war.

"Little Fag Thomas eating alone now?"

I said nothing.

"What, another fag ate your tongue?"

"Stop it, Sean." It was weird to hear him talking like that. It was like, you know, like it wasn't him.

"You tell everyone that you've been lying, that you betrayed our friendship, you betrayed the team.

Tell them or else . . . " Sean sounded like me somehow. The *me* I become sometimes.

"I already told you I'll say what you want me to say if that will make you happy, but . . . "

"No buts. I want you to tell the truth. I want you to tell them that we were friends, nothing else. Tell them that we have never been together, that you tried to kiss me like the faggot you are and . . . "

"And?"

"And that you are a fag and a bitch, a lying bitch."

Yeah, love brings out the worst in you. I mean, I have been called a fag so many times, but it's different when you're called one by precisely the one person you have fucking decided to love.

"Fag! Fag! Fag!"

All of a sudden, the whole cafeteria was coming toward us and they were all calling me fag, even those I believed were my friends, like the rest of the swim team.

"Fag, fag, fag. Fag, fag, fag, fag, fag, fag."

"Quit it!" Mary yelled.

"Fucking assholes, leave him alone," Ron added.

Mary grabbed my arm and she and Ron got me out of there.

"Fag has been rescued," someone yelled.

How can one syllable hurt so much? How can one syllable make so much noise?

"Are you okay?" Ron asked me.

"Of course he isn't okay," Mary said. "Tom, listen to me, ignore those fucking assholes." Mary held me in her arms. She was the first person in school I opened up to. She knew I was gay and she had always been supportive.

"Why are people saying that? Did you and Sean really . . . ?" Ron asked.

"Shut up, Ron, of course not. Right, Tom?"

I didn't have to answer. My face, my body, everything in me answered their questions.

"Fuck," said Ron.

"Oh, Tom—"

I didn't let Mary finish her sentence. Mary

had asked me directly if something was going on between me and Sean and I had denied it. I denied the truth to one of my best friends. I went straight to my locker and walked out of school. I skipped the last two periods and swimming practice. Got home, filled the bathtub. And you know the rest. The pills, the bathtub . . . my failure.

CHAPTER THREE
i stutter, i gay

For a long time, I didn't know I was gay. For starters, I always knew that I didn't like girls all that much, at least not in *that* way. And now that I think about it, I didn't like boys either. I guess I just didn't like anyone. I liked my books, my mom's necklaces, my Legos, and I liked swimming. I was just me.

It's like in *Billy Elliot,* the movie. He liked dancing without actually thinking about what it meant. He accepted his cross-dressing friend without thinking about what he was. I have probably watched *Billy Elliot* a thousand times. I only got away with it because we made a deal, mom and me. I would do what I was asked to do in all of my appointments with the speech therapist and I would be allowed to watch whatever I wanted. And all I wanted to watch was *Billy Elliot*. I watched *Billy Elliot* after every single one of my therapy sessions. I went to the speech therapist for almost a year, two times a week, so . . . do the math.

As a kid, I used to stutter. It's a thing that sometimes comes back when I'm nervous. If you think about it, in my life there have been two reasons to bully me: my stuttering and my fagging.

I hated therapy. I cried and cried before, during, and after the first few sessions. Mom would lose her patience and say, "Stop stuttering, Tom. Just stop it."

Dad was a bit nicer. He would simply ask, "Why don't you try to not stutter?" I would only cry, and this would lead me to stutter even more. My stutter went away thanks to Dad. He pulled me out of speech therapy. That was the first time, and only time so far, he challenged Mom.

The therapist's methods were horrible, exhausting, it was like doing weights with your tongue and your tongue alone. I hated it. I started crying, "I don't wanna go anymore, I don't. I hate it. I hate her."

Dad said, "Edna, this thing isn't working. The more he thinks he shouldn't stutter, the more he stutters." Dad realized that being too conscious about not stuttering made me stutter even more. So, as a way to distract me from it, he decided I should do stuff. Sports.

My old man became like Billy Elliot's dad: obsessed with his kid practicing a real man's sport. The problem here is that Dad is terrible at sports, so he asked his brother, Uncle Robert, to help, just as he did with Jeremy. My brother was on a soccer team so that's the first thing we tried. But just a couple of sessions taught us that soccer was not for me.

"Don't worry, there are lots of other things to try, right Robert?" Dad said.

Uncle Robert tried to persuade him, "Maybe sports are not for Tom, just like they weren't for you." But Dad ignored him and made me try everything. Football, baseball, basketball, karate, you name it and I tried it. All I wanted to do was stay home and watch *Billy Elliot* again or any of those *Cirque du Soleil* HBO specials, which, by the way, I loved to death. Instead, I had to practice some stupid sport.

Our basement ended up full of gear that I never used more than one summer. "Some kids just don't take to sports. Why not get him involved in your insects?" Uncle Robert suggested after witnessing whatever sport failure I had performed. There was no way Dad would let me near any insect. I was a threat.

He simply said, "Tom has the strength for sports, just like Jeremy. He just hasn't found *his* thing." I wonder if he actually believed it.

Anyway, you gotta hand it to him, not even once did the man quit trying—or let *me* quit. Uncle

Robert tried again to convince my dad to get me into insects. "Maybe he ends up liking them as much as you do," Uncle Robert said, and then Dad told him about the ant farm episode, so insects stopped being an option. The fact is, Dad really wanted me to find my *thing*. And I did, and when I did, I also found my other *thing*. But that's a different story.

Of the two of us, Jeremy is the athlete. Jeremy actually likes sports and is great at all of them. He's on the soccer team of his school in Montreal, Les Carabines. Not that he has told me about it, but he keeps posting pics of his games and shit on his Facebook. He writes about it, too. He writes mostly in French so I have no fucking clue what exactly goes on in his life. Like Dad, he liked insects too. He didn't like literature all that much, like me and my mom. I had never thought about it that way but he is really more like Dad, and me, well . . . I'm my mother's son, no doubt. A total bitch.

When my brother left, Dad became more of a closet Dad to me. I mean, he never stopped going to my practices or competitions, but you could see how things were different for him. You see, he and Jeremy used to hang out a lot, sometimes Uncle Robert would go along. Camping, hiking, shit that I would never do even if they paid me. When they were away for a weekend, life was simple. Mom would stay in her room, reading, watching TV, or would go out with her friends and leave me money for pizza. I could do whatever I wanted, like watching *Billy Elliot* or "checking" out Mom's Sears catalogues.

Anyway, I'm sure Dad really did know about me since I was a kid. He just didn't have the guts to admit it to himself. It's like too much. This world—the gay world, I mean—had no a place in his.

"Why would a woman prefer to be with a woman?" he said once. That's what he would say whenever he faced anything remotely gay, like the *Will and Grace* re-runs on TV, or mom's hairdresser.

I've considered talking to him about it, you know.

To Dad, I mean. Right after our Sunday swimming practice. This is how it would be:

"Dad, I need to tell you something." Or just simply, "Dad, I'm gay."

Dad would look at me and say, "Why don't you just *stop* being gay?"

Sean told me once he would never dare to open up to his parents. I guess he has his reasons, God being one of them. You see, Sean's family is super-Christian, the Christianest ever. And he grew up hearing that being gay is not only a sin but also an evil thing. Of course, Sean isn't stupid, but he respects his parents' beliefs.

Sean's mom is a sweet lady; she's like the perfect housewife, or maybe any mom is the perfect house-wife compared to my mom. His dad is different, he's an actual *dad,* one of those who preaches and cares and argues and that's it. If only he was a little less obsessed with all the Christian stuff, that's *his* failure. My dad? I think he's a *total* failure.

* * *

There's this song by Antony and the Johnsons, "Fistful of Love." I listen to it all the time, but tonight, tonight the fucking song is my anthem. There's a part that says, "And I feel your fist and I know it is out of love." So true. Sean's fists on my face were hitting me out of love.

By opening my mouth, not only did I threaten the normality of his life, I killed our relationship. Isn't it funny? I killed my relationship in just one try, but I have failed at killing myself every single time I tried.

I have spent the last couple of hours thinking about walking to his house. Maybe we can talk? Maybe we could fix things. *Falling for Sean was a mistake*, I tell myself. I should have kept things the way he wanted them. He would still date Hanna and go to church and ride with me and our friends. We would sneak out of swimming practice to make out here and there or text all day long. All of that's impossible now. Many guys are together by pretending they are not together. That's how it works all the time.

I'm sick of checking Facebook every five minutes. I tried reading our old conversations but I know it will only make me feel like an idiot. I turn my computer off. I lay on my bed and turn on the TV. *Skins* is on. I watch the episode when Maxxie, the gay guy from the group, ends up having sex with a neighbor who used to kick Maxxie's ass. I'm so tired but I just can't sleep. I keep picturing Sean trying to get me out of his car, yelling at me, hitting me.

CHAPTER FOUR

swim, tom, swim.

FINALLY FELL ASLEEP ONLY TO WAKE UP AT FOUR A.M. WITH the TV still on. It's a surprise Mom didn't come to yell at me. *Billy Elliot* was on. What are the odds? I started watching exactly at the scene that Billy starts dancing for his dad in the gym. Looking him right in his eyes, it's like he's saying, "Look, Dad, this is who I am and you better take it!"

I can't help it—*Billy Elliot* is still my favorite movie of all time. I remember once I gave Sean a list of reasons why I liked it so much:

1. Billy doesn't have a mom because she died. I don't have a *mom*-mom and sometimes I wish she would just fucking drop dead.

2. Billy is different. I'm different.
3. Billy likes dancing as much as I did, as much as I like swimming now.
4. Billy has a dumb big brother. I have one of those too but mine lives in Canada.
5. Billy's dad is like a macho dude who only sees life through boxing. My dad only sees life through sports (or insects).

Billy's dad sends him to boxing classes to make him strong. Does that ring a bell? When I mentioned swimming to Dad, he was the happiest man on earth and I went swimming with him for a whole week and then he even got me a private instructor.

Why swimming? Easy, because of Tim Gunn, a guy that's as important in my life as Billy Elliot.

* * *

Once I watched an interview with Tim Gunn. In case you don't know it, Tim Gunn is the old gay dude on

Project Runway (such a cliché, right?). Anyway he was talking about his teenage years and how he stuttered and how he wasn't into sports until he found out swimming was perfect for him. For starters: it's clean; you don't sweat; plus, in a way, it is a solitary sport. Think about it, even when you are on a swim team, it is all about you. You don't have to pass the ball or get shit from your teammates because you did or didn't do this or that. I mean, you do get shit from your teammates, but not as much as you do when you play football or soccer or basketball or . . .

I told my dad, "What about swimming? Can we try that?"

He smiled and said, "We sure can." I was maybe ten years old. I have been swimming ever since.

Swimming is just great. I have been on a couple of teams and have had a couple of coaches and no matter how mean they could get—both teams and coaches—it's when I'm swimming that I feel the happiest. Outdoor or indoor pools, lakes, oceans, you name it, swimming is just great. Flying must feel the same. You feel free. It's all about you and your arms and your body and you're not thinking about anything, just swimming.

I have heard professional swimmers say swimming is like escaping. I agree. You know, when you are swimming it's like you're escaping from your family, your problems, yourself. It became a kind of hiding place. I didn't realize I was trying to escape who I was, even though I didn't really know who I was. One thing I learned from Dr. Stevens is that there's no escaping who you are.

Anyway, then came the underwater writing. I don't know when or how it started. This is what I do, when I swim just for practice, I make stories, I write letters, I talk to people. It is like I get creative when I'm underwater. Sean told me once that when he started swimming as a kid he used to repeat the "Our Father" prayer under the water, one, two, as many times needed.

"I don't pray," I told him. "I write letters." He looked at me like he was trying to understand what

I was saying. "I do, I jump in the water and think, *Dear____*, and insert the name of the person I want to write to, and then I start. Underwater I 'write' whatever I want. It's great, you should try it."

Sean smiled and said, "You should 'write' to me." He was flirting.

I have to say that if I survived middle school it was because of swimming. I would go straight to the pool after class every single day. When you submerge, everything submerges with you and stays there. Your problems, your crazy mother, your fucking classmates, your whatever-it-is-that-you-feel. Everything. Gone. With every stroke.

Also, I must say that swimming is, in a way, the one thing Dad and I share and enjoy together. I know what you'll say: When you're swimming you don't get along with the other swimmer; you are on your own; you just swim and swim and swim, flip your turn, and go back to swimming. You're right.

At some point, while you are swimming, you stop for a second and look around, that's when you see he's there, your partner in swimming. In my case, sometimes that partner was my dad. Dad swimming with me. Hell, Dad swimming *for* me.

Anyway, when I joined Riverside's team, it took me a while to fit in. I think I should thank Sean for fixing that, because when I finally did, it was all fun. I was one of the boys, but at the same time, I knew it was all about me—about my speed, my strength, my resistance. I became very competitive. It isn't about winning; winning is just a matter of not wanting to be last, not wanting to be the joke again.

Everything was going great until I fell for Sean. Stupid Sean. Stupid swim team.

* * *

"Tell me what it is about swimming that you like so much?" Dr. Stevens asked me one day.

So I told him all about it.

He seemed to understand. "Well, it's good that you have that, right?"

My swimming. Yes, it's good that I have that.

We met three times a week for that whole summer. Dr. Stevens and I, that is. At first I would sit down with him without saying a word, just looking at my nails or my shoes or whatever, but not at him. He didn't lose his patience though; he would just stare at me. He remained. Then he was there, sitting next to me at the cafeteria. Breakfast, lunch, dinner, Dr. Stevens right there. He was also there during Friday night movies or picnics. He was everywhere. It's like he was saying: *You cannot escape from me.* And I couldn't.

I finally opened up, saying, "Just fucking leave me alone, why are you always here? Just let me be!"

He looked at me and said, "Is that what you want? Is that why you wanted to kill yourself? To be alone?" No, I didn't want to be alone. I don't want to be alone. That's what I learned with him. I stood there.

"No," I said.

"Of course not, who would want to?" Then

Dr. Stevens added, "How about some hot tea and a walk?"

I nodded, and then said, "I don't really like tea. Do you have hot cocoa?" He smiled. "With marshmallows. I have hot cocoa with marshmallows. The instant kind."

When I stopped playing games, Dr. Stevens and I started talking and talking and talking and talking over tea and hot chocolate with marshmallows.

Two lessons I learned:

1. Hot chocolate with marshmallows can save your life.
2. You must keep your promises.

I have always tried to rely on lesson one: if a hot chocolate with marshmallows cannot save your life, nothing can. The second lesson—well, I forgot to take it to practice when it came to Sean.

I'm a veteran in therapy. Yes, it all started with my speech therapist, but later in life, when I started to get into trouble at school and at home, Mom decided I had ADHD and needed meds and therapy.

Meds I didn't mind; what did I know? But I hated the idea of therapy. I asked, "Why do I need it?"

"You need someone to talk to, someone who can understand you."

"Isn't that what moms are for?"

"Don't get witty on me, Thomas. I mean, someone with credentials," Mom said.

She was right about not having credentials, for sure.

I cannot talk about my relationship with Mom because well, I've never had one. She regrets having me. It's not a guess. It's not something I say to myself to play victim, no. She has actually said so. She has always acted like she was the girl who had to leave everything because she was knocked up, as if she had to marry Dad and stay with Dad because of us, as if she had to be a mom because of us. But, hey, I was born second. I'm supposed to be the son she did plan.

Jeremy, my brother, he was the mistake, at least that's what she says "jokingly." Jeremy never said anything, not a word. He's like Dad, all quiet and shit, but I'm sure he was sick of Mom and that's why he left for Montreal as soon as he could. First, he went as an exchange student, and then he decided to stay for college. Dad didn't like the idea all that much; he and Jeremy had always gotten along pretty well. Jeremy and I have never really gotten along, except when we were kids.

It's weird though, because I've always had this hidden belief that if things got too rough with Mom I would go and live with Jeremy. He would take care of me, like he did when we were kids, like he did even after we stopped hanging out. Who knows? Maybe he'd say, "Yes, little brother. Of course, you can come."

We have this picture in our living room of Jeremy and I riding a go-kart. He's driving, I'm next to him, yelling, big smile on my face, arms up. Him? He's all serious as if he was in charge of driving us through the Rocky Mountains. He's a responsible driver; I'm a party animal.

Jeremy has also been Mom's punching bag, only

he wouldn't say anything. Me? She might slap or kick or beat me, but I always have something to say. Like that time when she found me singing karaoke dressed like Britney Spears. She pulled my ear and slapped me in the face, and I said, "Hit me! Hit me baby one more time!"

Of course this just made things worse. She slapped me again and pulled my hair. I kept saying it, I kept singing, "Hit me baby one more time."

Jeremy was there. He couldn't do anything, but he was yelling, "Shut up, Thomas! Just shut up!"

But I didn't, it was my moment. Needless to say I was not allowed to go out or go to the pool for one month. *One month.*

I was more careful after that. Being without swimming was painful. I felt like a fish out of water. I was dying!

Like I am now. I wish I were in a pool right now. It's like my whole body tells me, *Swim, Tom, swim.*

CHAPTER FIVE

sex sex sex

IGUESS YOU CAN SAY IT WAS MY FIRST SPORT. Masturbation. Yes, masturbation is a sport. I liked it. I liked it *a lot*! I did it whenever I could. I didn't think it was wrong; I didn't think it was a sin or some shit like that. I didn't think, period! I just did it. And did it. And did it. In the shower, in my bedroom, in the bathroom. Once in front on the TV watching the Olympics. A couple of times while checking out the people in underwear in the catalogs my mother got in the mail. I say *people* because that's what I thought, but I am sure my favorites were the male models.

Surprisingly, I was never caught. It's kind of

embarrassing to talk about it, but it is the only way to explain that my only experience with "sex" had been me and my hand. Me and my hand, me and my hand.

I didn't do it for a long period, though. Why? Well, mostly because of my ups and downs, and my meds. It was during that time that I started taking shit like Ritalin and Adderall. To all this, you have to add the mess that came after the Charlie Dale-Love-Letter Incident and so my hand and I took a break. Then came the teen mental clinic, where I didn't do anything. One, because of the meds I was taking; and two, because I was sharing a room with three other guys.

Anyway, once I got out and learned—accepted, realized, whatever—that I was gay, well, I started doing it all the time. By then, summer was almost over but it was still kinda hot. Things changed, though. One, I was not a kid. Two, I wasn't on any strong medications. Three, creativity. I added some imaginative shit to my—let's call it—*process.*

I shouldn't need to explain. As a kid I just did it without thinking. As a teen I did it thinking about guys. Guys like me. Guys like Pretty Face, this guy who worked at the supermarket. Can't explain it, but just seeing him gave me goose bumps. He was not handsome; he was pretty. Just pretty. He smiled at me once and talked to me twice. The first time he said, "Can I help you?" The second time he told me to have a good day. I'm sure he had a nametag but I can't remember it. For me he was Pretty Face, the protagonist of my fantasies.

* * *

When Sean and I were just friends, we used to talk shit all the time. Then talking shit turned into talking about ourselves. I opened up and told him all about Mom, Dad, Jeremy, my meds, my ups and downs, the clinic. He told me about his parents, summer camps, mission trips, and God, of course. He barely talked about his girlfriend and when he actually did, it sounded more like him talking about a pet, a cute, loving French poodle or something. It was kinda fishy. I started wondering, what was his deal with her, or with me? See:

1. We were together all the time—maybe not in school because in school he was either with Hanna or with his buddies, but . . .
2. We hung out before, during, and after practice.
3. Sometimes we even did stuff on weekends.
4. It was more like dating than hanging out with your best friend.

So, believe me, I had plenty of reasons to be confused. I began falling for him. At some point, Sean—well, Sean edged Pretty Face out of my bedtime stories. Sean became the object of my masturbation. That changed things. I started getting super-nervous about being next to him before, during, and after practice. I mean, if you are dressed, you are sorta okay—you can hide the pencil in your pocket. But, if you are in a Speedo, you are fucking screwed. The pencil cannot be hidden. So, when the pencil got ahead of me, I stayed in the pool just a little longer.

"Gentlemen, hit the showers," the coach would say. Everybody got out of the pool and grabbed a towel except me. I stayed in.

"Coming, Tom?" Sean would ask, and my mind was like: *I would love to. I would love to come—all over you.*

Sex was the main topic at the showers. Who would do who, who did who, who was about to do who? The best was: who would do this or that teacher. It was kinda funny. My way into these conversations was adding: "Oh, hell yeah, if I liked chubby, grumpy chemistry teachers I would totally do her," or, "Not even as a favor." Stupid shit, you know. Sean would just laugh and stuff, but he never said a thing about him and Hanna and no one gave a shit either. No one except for me.

One day we were in the showers and I asked him, "So, you guys don't have sex, do you? You and Hanna?" He stood there, washing his face, his hands covering his eyes. I pretended to be doing the same. I pretended not to care.

Then he turned off the water. My guess was that he would ignore my question. I was wrong. "No, we don't." Long, long pause before adding, "We won't."

I was like, *What the fuck?* "Won't? Really? Because you are Christian and you respect her and shit?" I was being an ass. I was rinsing my hair, eyes closed, so I did not notice that he was standing right behind me. I did not notice it was only us in the showers. I did not notice that he was staring at me. And when I say me, I mean my butt.

I finished, turned off the water and when I turned to get my towel I caught Sean in the act. In the act of checking me out. He played it off immediately and walked to his locker as I wrapped myself in a towel. Nothing happened, though. I mean, not *that* day.

* * *

Little by little Riverside became my favorite place on earth. It became a chance for me, an alternative for my life. New people, new teachers, new everything.

The best, though, was the swim team. At school I would hang out with Mary and Ron. I would see Sean after school. He would pick me up to go to practice, then he would drive me back. Sometimes, just sometimes, we would grab a snack before he dropped me off. That day was no different.

"I'm kinda hungry. Want some fries?" Sean said.

"Sure."

"McDonald's?"

"Where else?"

Instead of getting our fries and sitting down to eat on one of the tables outside McDonald's to see what people rented from the Redbox, Sean suggested we go for a ride.

"Are you driving up to Scenic Road?"

"Yeah, is that cool?"

"Yeah, yeah, it's just . . . nothing," I lied. It *was* something.

Like all cities, Riverside has a spot where people go to make out. A make-out point. But in Riverside, there's another spot that only a few know about. A different kind of make-out point. Yes, Scenic Road.

I had been there once, after I left the clinic and before things started between me and Sean. I had heard about what went on there, thanks to Lyla. "So, a friend of a friend was with her boyfriend— you know, trying to find a place to be 'alone.' They ended up at Scenic Road. Dude, that place is populated by gay people. Did you know that?" Scenic Road? Of course I didn't know about it, but the minute I did, I had to check it out. I was looking to hook up, but nothing. The only words I got there came from a mean old guy, who said, "Aren't you too young to be here?"

I gave him a look. "Aren't you too old to be here?"

He gave me a look.

I heroically gave him a finger.

The End.

That first day on Scenic Road with Sean, the big question was, *Why did he drive us here?* I was not going to play the fool, so I went all cocky and said, "Wow, Sean, naughty boy, why did you bring *me* here?" Believe me I was expecting everything but his answer.

"Why do you think, Tom?"

If this was a game, I wanted to play along.

"Dunno, you tell me. What are you up to? Ha ha," I said as I saw how we were going further and further down the road.

"I'm up for anything if you are," Sean said without looking at me.

"*Anything*? Be careful what you wish for."

"You be careful," Sean added while placing his right hand on my left thigh.

Our boomerang went back and forth. It stopped being funny. I was turned on. *Is this really happening?*

I thought. No, I didn't think about it, I said it, "Is this happening?"

"Only if you want it to," Sean said and took his hand off me.

A second later we were making out. Sean and I. It *was* happening. All of a sudden he stopped. I remember thinking, "This is it. He's kicking my butt out of his car." But no.

He just stopped and reached for my hair, caressed it and asked, "You won't tell anyone, right, Tom?"

"Not if you don't want me to," I said.

"Promise?"

"Promise."

Sean lifted up my shirt and started kissing my chest, my shoulders. His lips were everywhere, his hands were everywhere. I lifted his shirt and repeated the same moves.

It was the beginning of the fall. The best time of my life.

* * *

The following hours, days, and weeks we hung out just the same. No more, no less. To our daily agenda we added some "quality time" on our Scenic Road. Sometimes we even locked ourselves in his or my room, kissing, kissing, kissing. That's all we did. Well, not all, there was some touching here and there, some exploring . . . some . . . some more stuff that I can't even describe.

We had this game, the touching game. We would both take everything off but our boxers. One of us would lie down on the bed and the other one would walk with his fingertips all along the other's legs, arms, stomach, shoulders, face, the whole body. Then we changed places. Nothing happened beyond that, it was just a touching game. But I know we both wanted more. Pencils cannot be kept in pockets forever.

We exchanged Christmas gifts and *I-love-you*'s. We texted all day long. He started calling me Tom-Tom. We planned to keep things under the radar. He: boyfriend of the year. Me: gayest of gays. No one saw anything weird in our friendship because I still had my friends and he still had his. He was a sweet Christian guy who accepted all types of people in his life. I was his gay quota. Plus, he had a girlfriend and Hanna took me in as the gay friend all girls want. I even hung out with her and her friends at the mall sometimes.

Only Ron and Mary found it odd. Mary would make fun of me for hanging out with the popular people. "I'm just doing it for my team," I would say, "but I save the best of me for you two." We all laughed. The truth is that even though I hung out with Sean and his friends, I preferred being with my friends. Sean's friends were cool but so airheaded, unlike Ron and Mary who were smart as shit.

Everything was going great. I had time with my friends, time for Sean's friends, and time for Sean and me. Really, it was all great, I mean, at least in my life outside of home, because inside home I had to deal with all the same shit.

"You're going out, again?" Mom would say when she saw me all dressed up, keys in my hand.

"Yes, Mom."

"What about school?" she would ask.

"What about it?" I would reply.

"Well, don't you have homework?"

"Yes, I'll do it at Sean's."

"Who is Sean? Is he in your classes?"

"Sean's a sophomore who sometimes tutors me. He's on my swim team. I've told you about him. Dad knows him, right, Dad?"

"Mmmh?"

"You are not going anywhere!" Mom would yell.

Doors slamming, name calling, that's how the scenes always ended. Sometimes I managed to sneak out, sometimes I didn't. When I didn't, I would throw a fit and yell and cry. I would call Sean, crying, "I hate my mom. I hate her." Sean thought I was exaggerating.

So, except for those moments, everything was going great between Sean and me. Until we decided to have sex.

He planned it.

I accepted.

We did it.

Here's how it went down. His parents were going to be away for the weekend. He even asked his mom if I could stay with him and she called mine. My mother could not say no to a woman who was honored as Woman of the Year in the local newspaper. I wonder if she didn't find it odd. I mean, the last time I had a sleepover was like eight years ago and it did not end well. I had an asthma attack and ended up in the hospital. Mom said yes.

Sex was happening. Sex was finally happening.

I did not know exactly what we were going to do. I knew Sean's body, I had seen him in a swimsuit at least three-to-four times a week since we met. I had seen him naked, sorta, in the showers. I had seen him and touched him in his boxers. This time I was going to see him as a whole, just for me. I was nervous. The fantasies I had been building night after night would become real. They became real.

No, I'm not sharing any details about that

weekend, about our first time, but I can tell you this. The first time sucks. You really don't know what to do, you are both ashamed and horny, so horny that accidents can happen and all of a sudden you end up with sticky stuff everywhere. You do know what I mean, right? So the only thing to do is try again, try as many times as you can, fool around, kiss, lick, suck. Anything that turns *you* on can be used to turn someone else on.

The problem is that everything got fucked up between us after having sex. Why? Easy:

1. Because I fucking wanted to make it public and he didn't.
2. Because I went nuts and opened my mouth.
3. Because he got insanely mad and beat the shit out of me.
4. Because I wanted to die.

And that's what brought me to this point in my life. I fucked up with the man I love. I tried to kill myself, but then didn't. I'm a mess. Any questions?

CHAPTER SIX
the f word

SCHOOL SUCKS, NO MATTER WHAT.

But it *really* sucks because Sean and I fought. No one talks to me. No one even looks at me. Not even the teachers . . . but with teachers, who cares? I hate them all. Except Mr. Reynolds, who knows how to make history actually matter. I'm in his class when Miss Monroe, our counselor, comes and asks me to stop by her office whenever I can. When she leaves, the shit starts.

"Hey, you think Monroe needs some hair advice and that's why she wants Tommy?"

"Well, then she's made a mistake. Tommy isn't that kind of fag, or is he?"

Some assholes from class start babbling.

"Oh, please, stop. You're gonna make me cry," I say.

"What's going on?" Mr. Reynolds was setting up the projector on the other end of the classroom. That didn't stop them.

"Are you gonna cry? Poor baby, do you need a Prince Charming to comfort you?"

"Quiet down, kids."

"Yeah, he does. Such a shame princes don't like fags like him, boo hoo."

"Oh, *stop*. Don't hurt this FAG—please, please, please!"

"Thomas!"

As always, I should have shut my mouth. No teacher will allow the F word in class. Mr. Reynolds sent me to the principal's office right away.

I take my time. I go to the bathroom and I run into Ron.

"Hey."

"Hey, yourself."

"How are you? Mary and I are worried about you," says Ron.

"I'm fine, just fine. On my way to the principal's office."

"Why? Because of the thing with Sean yesterday?"

"No, got myself in trouble in my history class."

"Gee, that sucks."

"Yup."

Ron walks with me for a while, as slowly as possible. We say goodbye and before heading to the principal's office, I decide to go and check Sean's class. I have memorized his schedule so I know he's supposed to be in Lab. No sign of him. I finally make my way into the principal's office.

"Hey, Thomas, long time no see," his assistant greets me.

"Yeah, I guess I got tired of being a good boy."

She doesn't like my joke. I know because she gives me one of those looks, like my mom's, when she wants to punch my face but there are people around.

"What brings you here?"

"Mr. Reynolds sent me."

I hand her a note, which she reads only to give me one more of my mom's looks. Is it something that's being taught to all forty-something women or what? You know, how to shoot lasers from their eyes?

"Sit down. Mr. Brenner will be out in a minute. He's busy with a student."

I sit down when suddenly I recognize this student's voice. Sean. I can't understand what he's saying but it's definitely him. Sean in trouble? That's new.

* * *

The last time he was here was when Hector hit Sean's car. It was brand new and if it had been an accident, Sean wouldn't have done a thing. But Lyla, who told me this whole story, says that it wasn't an accident. Hector hated Sean's guts because of Hanna.

A classic high school love mess:

1. Hector and Hanna were sorta dating.
2. Hanna ended up being Sean's lab partner and fell for him.
3. Hanna stopped seeing Hector.
4. Hector hated Sean's guts.

The End.

I wasn't a student at Riverside High School yet. Lyla wasn't either, but she knows everything. She says she heard that the situation got wild, *wild!* Sean was pissed. Finally, Hector's parents paid for everything and Hector had to publicly apologize to Sean.

I'm there waiting for my turn with Mr. Brenner thinking about all that and at the same time wondering what's going on inside that office. Why is Sean there? I have to ask. I have to. "Is everything okay with Sean?" I use my sweetest voice possible.

"Don't be nosy, Thomas," she says, borrowing one of my mom's looks again. But then a funny thing happens—maybe because I said sorry, or maybe because I don't ask anything else, or maybe because I showed her my best *I'm-so-concerned* look, or maybe because I said, "I like your hair like that," or maybe simply because she was bored—but she adds, "What I can tell you is that Sean will not get away with it, Thomas."

"Not get away with what?"

Silence.

It seems that Sean is in trouble, and trouble is a word that one would never use when talking about him. How could you? This is the class president, the sports star of Riverside High School, model student, and model teenager, winner of math contests, and lead singer of his church band. The only son of the most loving couple of Riverside. Boyfriend of the most popular girl in our school. Sean is everyone's favorite person. I would actually hate him if . . . well, you know, if I didn't love him. He's honest, cool, friendly, responsible, humble—everything you would want in a guy. Except, he's gay.

So gay! This was good for me, of course, but not for everyone else.

As I said before, when I was a kid I didn't think

of myself as gay: I just knew that I wasn't like all the other boys. I knew what I didn't like. But Sean, Sean has always known he was gay. For some reason he ended up at this summer camp—wait, no, I must be accurate—this Christian summer camp, some sorta of Knott's Berry Farms for Christians. In this place, he and all the other kids his age were taught how to love God. And to love God it was necessary to talk about everything that was not godly. Like touching yourself, listening to rock, watching porn, or liking someone of your same sex. Especially liking someone of your same sex.

It was at this camp where Sean learned that what he felt and what he did with his neighbor, Steven Something, was forbidden. Sean understood then that he was gay and what he felt was wrong in a million ways. But he didn't "scrub" it off; he just decided to keep it to himself.

And to God.

Oh yes, Sean had told God about his being gay. God was the first person (or entity or power or whatever) Sean came out to. It is something to be proud of, I think. Sean believed that God wants people to love each other, period. According to Sean, God does not forbid same-sex love, He just forbids hate, deceit, and whatever else is in the Ten Commandments. "The rest," Sean used to say, "is just man's attempt to control what we do."

* * *

After a while, waiting for the principal at his office, I hear the telephone ring and it brings me back to reality.

"Yes, Mr. Brenner. Right away. Oh, Mr. Fischer is here, Tom Fischer . . . No, it was Mr. Reynolds who sent him . . . Let me see."

Here we go, I tell myself.

"Tom, Mr. Brenner wants to know if you have met with Miss Monroe."

"No. I mean, she asked me to meet her after class but . . . "

"No, sir, he hasn't . . . Okay, will do. Yes, I called Mr. Donovan. He said he would come as soon as he could."

Sean's dad was coming to school? I'm more and more intrigued now.

"Yes, right away," the assistant says. "Tom, Mr. Brenner wants you to talk to Miss Monroe."

"Now?"

"Yes, now."

"So, I'm not meeting with him anymore?"

"Not now, at least. Go to Miss Monroe's office. I will call and let her know you're on your way."

I'm so puzzled about every fucking thing that's happening that I don't even have time to be pissed off about meeting Miss Monroe, the stupidest counselor in the world.

∗   ∗   ∗

When I started going to Riverside High, I had to meet with Miss Monroe twice a month. Mom's idea. Before joining the swim team I would always go. It was a waste of time, but whatever. Once I joined the team, I started skipping some sessions.

One day she came to practice, she waited for us to finish and then approached me. "What is going on, Thomas? If you miss the next appointment, I will have to call your mother," she said. I told her it was nothing, told her I was doing okay, and that I was making new friends. "Still, you need to keep coming to see me."

Everyone saw me talking to her, but no one said anything. Except Sean, who asked me, "You going to counseling?"

"Yeah, kinda," I said.

"Why?"

Who asks that question? I guess Sean could tell I was uncomfortable but he kept on it.

"What do you guys talk about?" Sean asked.

"I don't know. Things." I went straight to the shower and left him there.

I was getting dressed; everyone had left by then,

everyone but him. He was bold now that I think about it. He sat down in front of me, and simply asked me *the* question,

"Are you gay?" he said. At first I didn't know what to say. It was weird, I didn't know where it came from, was it *that* obvious? I mean, by then, some people in school kinda knew. It took me a few seconds to say, "Last time I checked. Why?"

"I, I dunno. I'm sorry if I . . . I didn't mean to . . ."

"It's okay. I guess it's like asking me what my sign is."

"Mmhh, maybe. But, I, I don't believe in the zodiac and stuff," Sean said.

"You just believe in gays and stuff?" I asked.

He blushed. "Is that why you go to counseling?" Sean really wanted to talk about it.

"No." I said.

Then, he changed the subject. "How do you like the team so far?"

It was my second or third week on the swim

team. He actually became my first friend on it and, if it hadn't been for him, I would have never ended up being one of the boys on our team.

"It's cool. I like the coach. She's pretty badass," I said.

"Yup, but she can be fun too. I really like her. She's way better than our previous coach, dude. He was mad."

That's the thing with Sean—he's easy to talk to.

"Well, I bet he wasn't as bad as the one at my other school. He would make us practice at five a.m. in *winter*. A total Nazi," I said.

"Ha ha, you were at St. Mary's, right?"

"Yup, how'd you . . . "

"I saw you there, a couple of times. At those summer events that you guys organized."

I had never seen Sean before, which makes sense because all of my attention was in planning pranks with Charlie Dale. I couldn't help feeling flattered that Sean had noticed me, knew who I was. Of all the people, it was me he saw.

"Anyway, it's great to have you on the team. You'll sure help us win this year," Sean smiled at me.

Soon Sean and I were hanging out here and there. I fell for him immediately. It was merely platonic, though, I mean, he was straight, or was he? Since the beginning, I have been a bit shocked. Was he being friendly or was he flirting? I told myself, *Tom, he's just being nice to you. You are the new guy on the team.* Little by little our friendship became a bond. I mean, he still hung out with his own friends at school, and me with mine, but during and after practice it was all about us.

He was the only one who knows about my time at the teen mental clinic. He was curious about it and when he saw I was going through rough times because of my mom or because of whatever shit that bounced around in my head, he used to say, "Cheer up, Tom-Tom. I don't want you to end up at the clinic again. That would suck."

He made things easier for me. His liking me made the rest of the guys from the team like me too. I got invited to their pool parties and shit. Mary and Ron started making a little bit of a fuss about it.

"You don't hang out with us anymore," said Ron.

"I do."

"No, you don't. I kinda like that Lyla isn't around us all that much, but you—I miss you, man," said Mary, squeezing my cheeks.

"I'm sorry, it's just that the team . . . "

"The team this, the team that . . . Dude, what about us?" Mary said.

I meant it: I *was* sorry, but, at the same time, I felt no guilt. Being a part of the team made me feel like I belonged for the first time.

No. I am lying. The first time I felt I belonged was in the clinic. Is that pathetic? The swim team replaced the hole that I didn't know I had when I left the hospital. *That* clinic was like a home to me.

Yeah, I'm *that* pathetic.

* * *

You can't respect someone like Miss Monroe. How can anyone trust a counselor who has cats and kittens all over her office? Really, how? Cats, kittens, and motivational posters like, "Think positive!!!" Yes, with that many exclamation marks. Or, "Believe in yourself," or, "Be your best today." Cheesy, so cheesy.

As I sit in front of her, she asks me, "So, how have you been Thomas?" And she pushes her candy jar close to me.

"Not hungry," I say.

She smiles for like half a second and then says, "Why did Mr. Reynolds send you to the principal's office?"

Mr. Brenner's assistant is fast. Not only did she have time to tell Monroe that I was coming to her office but also about me being sent by my history teacher. I explain the whole situation to Miss Monroe. She gives me the eye.

"The way I see it," I say firmly, "You are responsible for that."

"Me?"

"Yes, if you hadn't come and asked me to meet with you in front of the *whole class*, no one would have made fun of me and I wouldn't have told them to fuck off."

"Language, Thomas."

"That's exactly what Mr. Reynolds said, and believe me, I wasn't the only one who was using the F word. Actually, they weren't using it—they were using the other F word."

"Which one is that?" she asks.

"Fag," I say.

"Thomas!" Miss Monroe is one of those people who is way too dramatic when they talk. You can almost see the exclamation marks flying.

"Well, it's true! You came to the class, two of my classmates made fun of me, and I responded. What else could I do?"

"Is this about *you* being gay?"

Miss Monroe is a tactful counselor, right? It takes me a few seconds to calm myself down and come up with a good answer, one I wish I'd written down—it was that good.

"It's more about the issues *everyone* seems to have with me being gay than me actually *being* gay."

She blinks at me, as if she has no clue what to say. But then she surprises me, "I'm sorry, Tom. You're probably right. It seems the rest of the world can't deal with an individual's choices. I mean, I know it isn't about choices but about being true to yourself, to who you *are*. Now tell me, is that what happened with Sean?"

"I . . . " I don't know what to say. Monroe is being like smart and shit. And I, I feel like I want to tell her everything: the whole shit.

A short summary of the last months of my life would look like this:

1. Sean and I were on the swim team, we hit it off, became friends and then one day he, well, he kissed me.
2. We were sorta secretly together, because of his

family and his friends and his girlfriend and his life and, and, and . . .

3. I wanted to be out. I mean, I wanted us to be out, out as a couple.
4. He didn't. "Not yet," he said.
5. After weeks and weeks and weeks of making out, of touching, feeling, we decided we wanted more.
6. We had sex.
7. Our first time, like all first times, I guess, was life-changing. I didn't want secrecy anymore. I wanted it all.
8. He still didn't want that. "No, not yet."
9. I opened my mouth.
10. He shut me the fuck out, a little too late though, and now he hates my guts.

But no, I don't share my list with Monroe. Instead I simply ask, "What do you mean?" *What does Sean have to do with anything?*

She brings the news, "We know Sean attacked you."

"No, he . . . didn't."

"Tom, we know *all* about it.

"But, how? Who . . . ?"

"Never mind that. What matters is that the situation is being addressed and you can stop worrying about Sean hurting you again."

Fucking shit, I think, or maybe I did say it. Sean is in trouble because of me, because of us. Mystery is, who ratted on Sean?

* * *

I text Lyla:

Have a question.

Thought u were mad, she texts back.

Mad?

Yeah, because I told Hanna about u and Sean

Oh that. Yeah, I'm mad, but whatever.

So what's your question

Who told the Principal about what happened in the cafeteria?

Lemme find out. Hold on

It takes Lyla less than five minutes to text back.

It was Hector

Hector?

Yup. Want me to find out why? Lyla is really the best source of information at our school.

It's kinda obvious, don't ya think?

For sure

Thx

Hey

What's up?

Are we cool?

For now. TTYL

K

There was only one reason why Hector would have opened his mouth to the principal: to get even with Sean. It's just like a fucking TV series—things at school were turning into a *Gossip Girl* episode.

CHAPTER SEVEN
the misfits

THERE'S A MOVIE CALLED *GIRL INTERRUPTED*, ABOUT a psych hospital where there are only girls. It all happens in the late 60s, early 70s, which is why I actually wanted to watch it. Well, in the movie, Winona Ryder ends up being part of a small group of troubled women in her ward.

That's how it was for me. I was part of a small band of troubled kids: Harry, Sarah and Julie, whose lives sucked like mine, and whose parents, grandparents, and stepparents also sucked big time. I didn't meet them right away. The first two weeks, I was a bitch who would not talk to anyone and sorta scared everyone away. Then Dr. Stevens came into the picture, and when I came around, he invited me to his therapy group.

"The Misfits is what they call themselves," he said.

"Oh, are you the shrink of a punk band?" I asked him.

"I guess you can say that," he said, smiling.

The Misfits were obviously not that old 70s band. The Misfits were Harry, Julie, and Sarah. And no, they were not the gothic-weirdo-scary kids I had seen around the clinic. The Misfits were formed by a cute blonde guy with *Threadless* T-shirts; a nerdy girl with big glasses, long braids, and super short bangs; and a tall redhead who looked like a young version of Tori Amos, my crazy mom's favorite singer.

"Hey, you're the one who pushed Fatty-Not-Slim Boy! Cool moves, dude," said Julie.

I said, "Who? I haven't . . . "

"No, butthead, you're confusing him with someone

else. This one did not push Fatty-Not-Slim Boy," said Harry.

"My name is Thomas and no, I didn't push any Fatty-Not-Slim Boy."

The three of them laughed, and then they said, "Hi, Thomas."

"Now this really is a support group, one where we get to introduce ourselves, like in AA and shit . . . " Harry said.

"Yeah, and at the end of each one of our sentences, Dr. Stevens will ask, '*And how does that make you feel?*'" Julie added.

Even Dr. Stevens laughed. It was a cool start. The Misfits were witty, funny, sarcastic, bitchy, dumb . . .

Who do they remind you of?

* * *

Life at the clinic changed after that. It changed because of The Misfits. I became one of them, one more butthead, which is what we called each other. I mean, I had always been one anyway. We hung out all the time, ate together, fought for the remote with the rest of the creeps around us, saved seats for each other on the field trips. Most importantly, we talked and talked and talked for hours. We got to the point where we even talked without talking. You know, gestures, looks, and shit would translate into: *Did you see that?* or, *Get the hell out of here*, which was Harry's favorite when he got to sit next to the Gothic girl he liked, or the brunette cutter who didn't say anything.

Harry was a Casanova, a Casanova UA, which stands for Underachiever. That was the nickname I chose for him because he never got to second base with any of the girls. Have I mentioned that he said I was not a Misfit but a Miss Fit? Ha ha, Harry was funny.

Not everything was great, though. After a month of being one of the Misfits, I got to see Sarah at her worst. Something on TV freaked her out and then she started talking nonsense, and, in like three seconds, she started hitting herself and saying who-knows-what about her mom and how she would end up like her. Then, she hit a nurse and a second later a whole team of nurses were holding her and taking her to a room where she was strapped to the bed.

We did not see Sarah for like a million days.

It sucked ass. It fucked us all up. And believe me, we were already fucked up. See:

1. Harry was in this place because, according to his parents, he had suicidal tendencies. But no, Harry was obsessed with sex. He was always touching himself, everything was sex, sex, sex for him. Then he got caught choking himself, so his parents thought, "Oh, he tried to commit suicide." But the choking thing was not a suicidal attempt but pretty much a masturbation exploration.

2. Sarah was a bit of a mystery. Something happened to her when she was a kid and

nobody knew what exactly. Something mom-related. She could be normal and cool and shit but she didn't like eating all that much. Sometimes she would lose her grip and it never ended well.

3. Julie was a classic cutter, not really sure why. She was terrified of many things and for that reason she had always been homeschooled. Her parents were hippies; her mom was cool, her dad not so much, but I guess you can blame them both for all her shit.

4. Me, well, I was just a boring teen with suicidal tendencies, but if you see teens' rate of mortality you would agree with me that I was completely normal despite what Mom thought.

Now I only keep in touch with Julie. Harry is now in juvenile detention, and Sarah, well, let's say Sarah is the only one who actually had the guts to do something to end her shit.

∗ ∗ ∗

Thinking about the teen mental clinic reminds me I haven't talked to Julie in the longest time, so I decide to call her. I need to forget everything that happened with Sean.

"Hey buttface," says Julie.

"Hey girl, how's it going?"

"Probably better than you."

"Why do you say that?" I ask her.

"You only call me when you feel like shit."

"Do I?"

"Yup."

" . . . "

"But no worries. I would pay to hear someone else's problems. Dude, I hate my parents. Can you believe I'm not allowed to use the computer more than an hour a day? Anyway . . . what's up with you?"

"I . . . I'm a mess, Julie."

"You? A mess?"

"I'm serious, Julie."

"What's his name?

I pause.

"Am I right or am I right?"

"Sean. His name is Sean."

"Which one is Sean, the swim team dude?"

"How do you . . . ?"

"I sometimes use my precious computer time to stalk people on Facebook."

"But you never post anything. I forget you are my FB friend."

"You actually forget I'm your friend at all. Ha ha. I think I'm a nobody on Facebook. Which is like being a nobody in life . . . "

"Yeah, I guess," I say.

"So, what about this Sean? Is he a dickhead?"

"No."

"He's not gay?"

"No. I mean, yes, but buried in like ten closets."

"He old?"

"He isn't old. He's just a year-and-a-half older than me."

"That is old, buttface. I tell you, gotta get freshmen, eighth graders or . . . "

"Or the homeless, I know . . . "

"Ha, ha, ha, I had forgotten about the homeless. So what happened with Sean?"

"Do you have time?"

"Do I have time? Lemme see, between my fucking homeschooling and my fucking dad who wants me to limit my social life to going out once a week, yes, I have time. Talk."

* * *

As always, talking to Julie helps. She makes me laugh. She empties my sack of shit. She says that if she ever finishes high school, which who knows when it will be considering she has been homeschooled for ages, she will become a psychotherapist or some shit like that. She's always been Dr. Steven's number one fan.

It's at the very end of our call when all the fun starts to vanish. Julie asks, "Tell me Thomas, did you try to do something?"

I don't answer.

"Fucking butthead, you did, didn't you?!"

I don't even have to answer. She knows. Julie always knows. She gives you a hard time, the kind you need, and then you open up.

"Julie, I—" I wasn't going to say anything. But I broke down. "I tried. I . . . It just didn't happen. I can't explain."

"What did you do?"

"It doesn't matter now. I didn't go through with it."

"And how did that make you feel?"

I laugh, she must be joking. But then she adds, "Seriously butthead, how did *that* make you feel?

"Dunno."

"Thomas . . . "

That should have been my first sign of alarm. Julie never, ever, ever calls me Thomas. To her, I'm butthead.

"Thomas, you can't play with this. You can't. I know we don't talk all that much but you are my rock. I can't go through this again, not again . . . "

"What're you talking about, Julie? Go through what? What does this have to do with you?"

"Everything. I couldn't bear seeing one of you going back to the TMS or worse."

"One of us?"

"One of my Misfits. I can't. I still think of Sarah all the fucking time and . . . "

"Relax Julie, I . . . "

"Is Sean worth it?"

"Worth what?"

"Worth being analyzed, sent back to the clinic, worth leaving everything behind, worth being tied up and observed all the fucking time because you are under a suicidal tendencies file! Is *he* worth it? Dying—is Sean worth you dying?"

I have no answer.

"Fucking idiot. That's how it all starts. You should come down and see me."

I think, *Yes, I should, I should go see Julie, spend a weekend with her, talk all night like the old times.*

Julie and I hang up, but the question remains in my mind.

Is Sean worth it?

I try to play with myself. A short affair with my hand with Sean as a movie playing in my mind. But I can't, it just doesn't work. I'm a mess.

CHAPTER EIGHT
cry me a river

AFTER MY UNSUCCESSFUL ATTEMPT TO SEX MYSELF, Mom gets home. I start hearing her concert of pots, pans, and "fucking shits." I'm waiting for her to yell, "Thomas, dinner is almost ready!"

I know the drill. I will go, set the table, we will all sit down, talk like half a sentence each one of us, and then, "Thank you. It was delicious. Night." It does not happen.

The telephone rings and I let her get it. I'm way too busy checking on the Facebook status of everyone in Riverside High. But there's no more mention about what happened in the last couple of days. No jokes or anything. My five minutes of fame have come and gone.

I decide to write something, the wittiest post on earth. I'm there, waiting for my muse to come and dictate the words when Mom comes into my room.

"What the fuck did you do?"

"Me?"

"Yes, you. What the fuck did you do? Can't I just have a moment of peace?"

I have done quite a few things lately, so, really, I have no idea which one of my deeds she's talking about. My question-mark face makes her explain.

"I got a call from Julie's mom."

She and my mom are not friends. They only have one thing in common—idiot kids. What could she say that has made Mom so pissed off at me?

"You tried to kill yourself again?" Mom yells.

That's it. The Thing. It's impossible; I can't believe Julie opened her mouth. No, not Julie.

"I don't know what you are talking about," I say.

"You don't know what I'm talking about," she repeats.

"Seriously, I have no clue."

"You have no clue."

This is one of my mom's habits: when she's mad, which is almost all the time, she repeats what you say.

"No, I have no idea."

"You have no idea."

"If I had tried to kill myself would I be here so calm and easy?" Calm and easy—yeah, right. "Would I be messing around with my . . . "

I do not even get to finish my sentence before my mother closes the lid of my laptop and slaps me. I hadn't had one of them in a long time. Slaps are my mom's trademark.

"I'm sick and tired of you, Thomas. *Sick* and *tired*. I cannot go through this. Not now. Who the fuck do you think I am?"

Slap.

"Mom, you don't really want me to tell you what—"

Slap.

Two slaps in a row. My face burns.

* * *

What happened was that after Julie and I hung up, well, she was moved or something and she fucking ended up crying and losing it a little. So, no, Julie did not mean for my mom to find out, but she was stupid enough to open up to *her* mom, the only person in her family who she actually likes. Julie's mom is one of those women who do feel concerned about people in this world and she decided to call my mom and advised her to check on me. The way I see it, more than worrying about *me*, my mom was troubled because someone *else* cared about me or knew about me or whatever. You never know with my mom.

"I am putting an end to this, Thomas. This time you better pull yourself together," Mom says.

Putting an end to . . . an end to my wanting to end? I think. It makes no sense, so I ask, "Putting an end to what, how?"

"I am sending you to a place where they will actually help you."

For a second I think about it. It wouldn't be too bad of an idea.

"Fine, send me back to the clinic. At least Dr. Stevens has more motherly instinct than you."

Slap number four.

"You little shit. Forget about Stevens and his methods. Forget about his clinic. I am locking you up in a mental hospital."

"No fucking way," I say. "No fucking way. I have school and the team and—" I almost say it, *And I have Sean.*

* * *

Whenever someone asks me about my mother I don't know what to say. Let me rephrase that. When a *therapist* asks me about my mother, I never know what to say.

I remember there was a time when I was in and out of the hospital. I don't know how many times or how many nights there were but it seems like I was there my whole kindergarten life. Mom was there. Always. Right next to me. She would be either on her phone or her laptop doing homework. That means she was there but elsewhere. I was connected to who-knows-what and getting shots and meds and all kind of stuff while she was learning her Hemingway and Faulkner and shit, but she was there, or sorta there.

I remember crying my guts out because I had to eat only boring, ugly-tasting stuff or because I had to get another shot or keep that oxygen tube up my nose and she would only say, "Hush, my Tommy, hush." And then she was back to her reading, writing. That's the only time I was Tommy. Fuck you, Hemingway, fuck you Faulkner, above you both, it was me. I was *her* Tommy.

But then as the *ins* and *outs* to the hospital started accumulating, she got sick and tired of me, of *my* being there on a bed and *her* missing school life. She was grumpy all the time, she stopped caressing, and she stopped caring. She would yell at me when I cried or complained or breathed. Anyway, during all that time that I was in the hospital, she missed classes, conventions, conferences, readings, she missed her school life because of me. Not that I knew it then, but she has managed to remind me of that every time she can. In the end she didn't even finish grad school and she became an English teacher at an all-girl's school. Something my brother and I should be thankful for because we never had to be her students.

Then it happened. I heard her on the phone talking about me as I lay on my hospital bed. She probably thought I was sleeping.

"Yes, in the hospital again, goddamnit. Thomas

is sick again. Believe me, I'm done with all this and his fucking asthma."

To this day I have no clue who she was talking to, but the rest of the conversation introduced me to a totally different person. Mom started talking shit about me and Dad and my brother. Mom started saying how sick she was of us all, and how stupid, stupid, stupid she had been.

"I mean, you are young and stupid, stupid, stupid and end up pregnant. What do you do? You get married and live with it. And when you get the guts to leave, what do you do? You go and fuck it up and end up pregnant again, and then, you're unable to leave."

You may think I was too young to understand, but I wasn't. I understood. That is the day I met my mother; the other one. The woman who was taking care of me was just a visitor who left and never came back.

That night I cried my guts out. I took the oxygen tube out of my nose, thinking that would kill me. It didn't. I failed, as always. A nurse put it back. I'm sure she thought it was all a mistake.

* * *

Thinking about all this makes me think of Dad and what he did when it was his turn to take care of me. He would sit down next to me, right on the bed— something my mom would never do—and read about the lives of insects all the time. I hated them, so I would tell him, "I don't like them, Dad. I don't."

"So what are we going to do then?"

"Tell me again about the centipede that wanted to be a ballerina or about the fly who wanted to be a flight attendant."

"Well, those are insects, too."

"Yes, but they are pretty." I said. Dad smiled and started telling my favorite stories.

My dad's stories were the best. Now that I think about it, even with insects I was so gay. If I ever come out to him I will tell him it is all his fault for telling me these stories.

* * *

"Did you hear me? I don't want to fucking go anywhere. You can't force me."

"Oh, cry me a river! I'm not asking you, 'Hey Thomas, do you want to go to this place so someone fixes your goddamned mind?' You're going. That's my last word," Mom tells me.

We keep yelling at each other. She pushes me around. I stand there as if it doesn't hurt. We are spitting shit at each other when all of a sudden something happens. Dad, *my* dad comes into my room. *My room.* "You are not sending him anywhere, not this time, Edna," he says firmly.

Dad yelling. Dad standing up to my mom. My dad. My dad.

* * *

At home we have this picture. You know, the classic family picture you display in your living room. In it, you can see Mom, Dad, Jeremy, Candy our dog, and me. We are all there together next to a Christmas tree at Grandma's. I mean, we are all there but none of us is there. See:

1. My mom has her hands on her shoulders, sort of fixing her blouse, looking down at it.

2. My dad does look at the camera, his eyes stare straight into it, but you can easily see that he's not there. His mind is probably travelling to the miniature world of insects or something.

3. Jeremy is looking down, either at Candy or at me.

4. Me? My eyes are semi-closed but my hand and my attention is on Candy, I'm feeding her a cookie or some other shit, who knows.

This picture is the best example of what my family life was like. We were together but we were not together. Christmas, New Year's, Thanksgiving, you name it. We were there but not there.

Just a few examples of our bonding:

"Pass the gravy."

"Did you feed the dog?"

"The plumber came today, he fixed the pipe."

I know. I'm almost sure that all families end up like this but I'm also sure that they have a past, a sweet little past when things were different, when there were laughs and jokes and something more than, "Pass the gravy." This isn't my family's case. We have always been like that. I guess that's why Grandma stopped inviting us over for family reunions. Cousins and uncles and aunts did not like us all that much.

Neither did we.

By the way, that's on Mom's side of the family. Dad's side is a whole different story. Yes, we were the weirdos, too, but they kept asking us over. But we never went. The only person from Dad's family that was somehow close to us was Uncle Robert. Uncle Robert was Dad's best friend.

The car broke down and my uncle was there with

Dad, helping out. If we were practicing any kind of sport or participating in any kind of competition, Uncle Robert was there. When my parents went out of town, Uncle Robert would babysit. He is the only person I know who can make Dad laugh.

My mom hates him, of course.

Anyway, except for Uncle Robert, it seemed that we were alone in this world. Not that it mattered, but it also seems that even inside of our own home we were all alone. Dad in his studio, Mom in the kitchen or in the dining room grading papers, Jeremy and I in our room when we shared one, or in each other's room as we grew up.

Yeah, that picture really describes the kind of family we are.

* * *

Tonight, right in front of my eyes, Dad has turned into some kind of Hulk, all green and shit, and he tells her she isn't going to send me anywhere. He tells her he's tired of her fucking ways of dealing with me, with us, all of us. He says, "Do you wanna lose Thomas like you lost Jeremy, is that what you want? No fucking way I will let you do this."

"But you don't know . . . " Mom babbles, but he interrupts her again,

"I know, I do know, Edna. I know you believe Thomas is as sick as you are, but he isn't, you are making him sick. You are driving him crazy."

Dad grew some. Mom babbles who-knows-what, gives me one of her looks and leaves the room saying, "This isn't over."

I wonder what Dad means? Mom, sick?

CHAPTER NINE
where have you been?

"WE ARE GOING TO MONTREAL," DAD SAYS.

"Montreal?" I ask. "What the hell are we gonna do in Montreal?"

"Spend a few days with your brother," Dad says. My brother, yes, I keep forgetting I have one of those and that he lives in stupid Canada.

"But I can't go to Montreal, I have school and . . . "

"No, you don't. Spring break, remember?"

All the fucking shit around my life has made me forget about spring break. No shit. That's why everyone was going crazy at school.

"What the hell am I going to do in Montreal?"

I say as I turn my back to Dad and sit down at my desk. I open my computer.

"What the hell will you be doing here?" Dad says as he closes my laptop. "Would you prefer to stay here and listen to your mother talk about admitting you to another freaking hospital?"

No, I did not want that.

"Start packing. I'll call Jeremy and buy tickets," he says before leaving my room.

I stayed there on my chair, thinking about the whole thing. The fight. My dad. The trip. I didn't want to go. I wanted to stay and try to fix things with Sean. I wanted to stay and figure out what's next for me . . . but . . . on second thought, maybe it's the best thing to do.

Montreal means going away. And right now all I want is to disappear. Forget all the fucking mess I made and obviously I want to be far, far away from my fucking mother.

For the first time in my life, I try to be an

obedient son to my father and start packing, not without posting it all on my Facebook wall:

Montreal, here I come. Isn't it awesome when you can just leave?

Ten minutes later I have twenty-five *likes*. Not bad, right?

I'm busy with my packing when my computer starts to beep. Facebook message. *Holy shit*, I think. *Sean, maybe?* But no, it isn't Sean. It is Mr. Jeremy Fischer, my brother. He typed, Hey. You there?

Yeah. What's up? I reply.

Dad just called me. Is it true? Are you two coming up here?

Seems that way.

It is probably the first time that my brother and I chatted. I ask him, Is it cool?

Yeah, yeah . . . it's just. Weird I guess. But yeah, cool. So when are you arriving?

Dunno, but we will be spring breakers Canadian style.

Ha.

Not only is this the first time I have exchanged messages with my brother, it is almost the first time we have talked at all. Or so it feels.

Our conversation goes on and on for like an hour. I think of Billy Elliot. I think of that moment when he tries to talk to his older brother in his room and nothing. At least I'm getting *something*.

* * *

Uncle Robert drives us to the airport. Of course, Mom would not drive us, she doesn't even leave her room to say goodbye. I text Sean one last time and then turn off my phone for, like, about twenty minutes. He does not text back so I really turn it off. I promise myself not to turn it on during our whole trip.

Dad explains to the flight attendant that he and his son are flying to Montreal. "No we are not checking our bags," he says. In that very moment I realize it has been years since we have traveled together, him and me. It feels good. I feel as if I'm a kid escaping with his dad. Or something like that.

The flight is long, long, long. Because I didn't get much sleep the night before, I take like a four-hour nap while flying. I dream of Sean, I dream of our weekend together. Dreams are the reality you really want, but I guess they can also be what you fear the most.

The feeling that I'm drowning in the depths of an ocean wakes me up.

"Are you okay?" asks my dad, he's almost done with his book *Ants, Bees, and Tree Bugs*.

"Yeah, it was just a dream," I say.

"Seemed more like a nightmare."

"Maybe." I spend the last hour of the flight wondering if I have done or said anything while sleeping right next to Dad.

We go directly from the airport to a hotel. My brother said he would meet us there. He lives in a dorm so I guess it will also be a treat for him to be away from his frat buddies or whatever. Dad has been here a couple of times so he's telling me all about the city as we ride in the cab. Montreal is fucking beautiful. No wonder my brother does not wanna go back to our Midwest town of seventy thousand people.

Seeing Jeremy is weird. He seems older and I just saw him during the holidays, but I guess that time I didn't pay attention, much less hang out with him. Besides, it was the peak of my relationship with Sean. Jeremy is in the lobby when we arrive. Dad hugs him and they pat each other on the back. When my turn comes along I don't know what to do. I go blank. *How do we do this every time we see each other?* I wonder.

In the end, we give no hugs, but just say, "Hey," to each other. But then it happens, he squeezes my shoulder. It feels nice. On our way to the room Jeremy shares his good news,

"I got tickets for *Cirque du Soleil.*"

"The what?" Dad asks.

"*Cirque du Soleil,* Dad. You know them. Mom

went with her friend Elizabeth when they were in Chicago, remember?" I say, but Dad has no clue.

"How did you get tickets?" I ask Jeremy.

"It was pure luck. My roommate bought them for his girlfriend, but they are saving for some trip and—anyway he sold them to me."

Cirque du Soleil! I'm fucking thrilled.

"It's tomorrow night. The only problem . . . "

I knew it, shit, I knew it. Life is against me as always.

"The only problem is that I have only two tickets, we can try to see if we can get a third one but . . . "

"You guys go. I don't even know what it is," says Dad. "I'll be fine. We'll spend the day together, have a nice dinner out, and then you guys go to your play."

"It's not a play, Dad."

"Whatever it is, you guys go," Dad says.

I want to say, *Thank you, thank you, thank you.* I want to jump. I want to yell. Instead I simply say, "So, that's tomorrow. What are we doing tonight?"

Dad looks at me as if I'm out of my mind. "How about room service and TV? I'm tired." Stupid jet lag.

I must have looked like a puppy, desperate to go out and pee because my brother says, "Well, there's this thing with my friends. Wanna come?"

I don't even think about it. Of course I want to go out.

I remember a trip when our parents took us to Chicago. It was either summertime or a spring break, I don't know. I just remember we had to stay in the hotel the whole time because of the craziness of Chicago's weather. A huge storm pretty much kept us from doing anything. All I remember from that vacation was swimming in the pool—which, thank God, was indoors—and room service. My favorite: a club sandwich, fries, and a coke. Breakfast, lunch, dinner—I could eat it all the freaking time. Maybe my parents argued, maybe it was boring, maybe it was the worst vacation ever, but in my memory it remains the best time of my life.

I am in Montreal, far from Mom, far from the possibility of going to a mental hospital, and far from the mess I created between Sean and me. For a few minutes, I feel almost happy. I already have my answer before Dad asks, "What do you want from room service?" We order three of the same thing. Comfort food.

* * *

When Jeremy was in tenth or eleventh grade, he had a girlfriend, Emily. She was cool. Unlike my brother, she talked a lot, and she was pretty, but more than that, she had a fun personality. I could see why my brother loved her. She made my dad uncomfortable with her many questions about the insects Dad studied, but he liked her all right, or at least it seemed so, because he always gave money to Jeremy, saying, "Here, take Emily out."

Mom hated Emily's guts. She didn't like that they hung out together so much or that she came to our house every other day. Jeremy, he just kept at it. Those were the shittiest times for Jeremy and the best times for me. You see, all of Mom's attention went into making Jeremy's life miserable so she didn't mind me hanging out with Charlie Dale, before the Letter Incident that is.

Jeremy and Emily started having sex. I heard that from Charlie who heard it from his sister who was Emily's friend. We were watching some shit on TV and Jeremy was getting ready to go out against my mother's wishes, so they were arguing.

"Your brother is doing it with Emily," whispered Charlie.

"You think?" I asked.

"I don't think, I know he is. My sister told me. They did it in your dad's car."

And my brother could have done it so many more times in my dad's car, and my brother could have stayed together with Emily, and my brother maybe even wouldn't have gone to Montreal if I hadn't told.

What happened was simple. At some point Mom got tired of arguing with Jeremy about his girlfriend and her whole attention was focused on how much time I was spending with Charlie and my way of getting her off my back was telling her that Jeremy and Emily did it all the time, even in our house.

Imagine the scene. Mom went crazy.

I hadn't thought of that whole Emily incident till now, when Jeremy and I were in Montreal, on our way to a party. Does Jeremy know it was me who dropped the dime on him? Probably not. I never felt too guilty when it all happened. Man, I had my own shit and, well, if you think about it, the whole episode with Charlie and the letter became my karma.

"So, how are you?" Jeremy says.

"Okay, I guess. You?" I ask.

"I'm okay."

"Cool."

It starts exactly like one of the conversations at home during dinner. You know, two, three words per person. Or so I think.

"Tom, seriously, how are you? Dad seems really worried about you."

This catches me off guard. What does he actually know?

"I'm . . . I'm okay."

"I know we never talk and I understand if you don't wanna, but you know, I'm here for you."

What was he trying to do?

I don't say anything, and then all of a sudden he asks the driver to drop us off.

"Here?" the driver asks. "Weren't you going to . . . "

"Here is fine. We'll walk."

What is going on?

As soon as we get out of the cab, Jeremy barks, "Listen, Tom. Life has taught me to mind my own business. I know you have your life and I have mine, and it has always been that way in our family, but maybe, just maybe, that's why we are all so fucked up. Maybe that's why *you* are so fucked up."

I want to punch his face.

"Me? I'm the one who's fucked up? You walked out on us, from our family."

"Jesus, Thomas. Tell me, who's our family? A mean, crazy woman, a man who has no clue of anything but insects, and a kid who . . . "

"A kid who's a fag. Say it. Just say it."

"I was not going to say that."

"You weren't, seriously?"

"No."

"What were you going to say then?"

"A kid who is too afraid to live. A kid who is a bitch to everyone."

"What the fuck are you saying?" I ask.

"Thomas, I'm sick of finding out you hurt yourself this way or the other," my brother said.

"I don't know what you are talking about, that only happened one, maybe two times," I say, all sure of myself.

"You are fucking kidding me, right? Do I have to make a list for you?"

"Be my guest."

And then Jeremy starts.

My list includes:

1. Trying to kill myself with pills, one, two, three times.

2. Opening my mom's car door while she was driving.

3. Cutting my wrists.

4. The latest, trying to drown myself.

I had never seen it that way. I had completely forgotten about the car and about cutting my left wrist and about the actual first time I tried taking pills.

"We shared a room for—how long? Also, we were always in the same school. What I'm trying to say is that I was there, I either saw or heard what you were up to."

"You saw what?" I ask him.

"I saw how either people pushed you away or

you pushed people away. Why? Because you were different."

"You mean gay."

"Listen, Tom, you can be whatever you want, but your issues have little to do with your being gay."

"I was bullied all the time, they called me a fag even before I realized I was one. Even Mom."

"I understand that, but you haven't helped either. I mean, yes, Mom gave you hell all the time, I'll give you that . . . But, you did the same—to everyone around you: me, Dad, people at school. Even before the Charlie Dale thing. You bitched out with everyone."

"What the fuck are you talking about?"

"Thomas, you push everyone away. You are a lot like Mom. You hurt people. You don't realize how mean you can be. And you even seem to enjoy it. You enjoyed telling Dad to fuck off when he tried to help you out of speech therapy and from every other therapy Mom sent you to. You enjoyed every time you earned one of Mom's slaps for talking back. I mean, you probably even enjoyed telling her about me and Emily."

"You know?" I ask, ashamed.

"Of course, I know," Jeremy says calmly, "and I wanted to kill you, but in the end, you did no harm. I just kept things with Emily a secret, but that's a different story. See, Tom, you feel good every time you hurt someone, it's like it makes you feel alive, at least for a while, then you realize what you did and . . . "

"And what?"

"And then you do stupid shit, like trying to kill yourself. You see, you don't actually go through with it."

"Because I'm a failure, I can't even do *that* well," I said and started crying. Jeremy held my shoulders and said, "No, it's not because you're a failure.

It's because deep inside, you don't want to kill yourself. You want to kill some part of yourself. But it has to stop. You have to stop. You are breaking Dad's heart."

Jeremy's words are blunt and horrible and at the same time so fucking real. That is exactly what happened with Sean. I hurt him. I hurt him first. Mouthing off was no accident. I knew what I was doing.

Part of me wants to make Jeremy eat his words, part of me wants to punch him real bad. Part of me feels broken. How is it possible? Still, I want to have the last word.

"Dad's heart? Dad has been no dad to me or to you. He got rid of you, didn't he?"

"Dad helped me out. He brought me here. Dad brought *you* here. Dad fought as much as he could so you wouldn't have to go to that fucking center again, like he did the first time you were there."

"Dad doesn't know anything about me. He doesn't know I'm gay."

"Yeah, Tom, he knows. He has always known, he just can't acknowledge it. He has no clue how to deal with it because that's the way he is, but he's been there for you, for me."

"Dad?"

"Yes, Thomas. Where have you been?"

"This is Mom's fault then, as always. It's because of her that I am who I am."

Jeremy looks at me and says, "It isn't as easy as that. Yes, our parents shape our lives, but in the end, it's up to us, you know? We decide whether we follow their example or go our own way."

I stand there, clueless about what to say. It's like Jeremy has become my brother again and not the kid who happens to be my brother.

"You hungry? How about Tim Hortons? They have the best doughnuts on earth."

We spend the rest of the night talking shit. I even tell him a little about Sean. I don't tell him all, of course. I feel different. I know it sounds stupid, but I do. It is like he introduced me to my own story, a totally different one. The bullied was actually a bully. Yes, it is time. Time for me to take my path.

When we arrive at the hotel, Dad is already

sleeping. He took the sofa bed and left the beds for us. Oh, Dad.

Jeremy takes a shower. I just lie in bed, thinking. I can't wait to see Sean and tell him all about this. I want to be honest, open up. I want to apologize, truly apologize to him.

I fucking miss Sean.

* * *

This morning we did a couple of things with Dad. He made us walk around downtown for an eternity. Then, we had a delicious brunch at this fancy place we found on St. Catherine Street. The French Canadians know their shit when it comes to food.

Now Jeremy and I are waiting for the *Cirque du Soleil* show to start. They are presenting *Quidam*, which I had already read about. The story is about Zoë, a girl who is, like, totally ignored by her parents. Life has lost meaning to her until she immerses herself in the imaginary world of Quidam.

It doesn't take too long for me to see myself in Zoë. I too have felt alone and lost. I too have parents who are more into themselves, although now Jeremy has introduced me to a different Dad. Still, Zoë's life is my story. Zoë uses her imagination to escape from her reality. I use my imagination the same way. Failing has never felt so beautiful.

I can't help myself and I start crying. I'm sure I'm the only one crying. I'm probably a joke to everyone at the theater, but I don't care and neither does Jeremy, who squeezes my shoulder again and again. I think of Sean, how I wish he was here, how I wish he could learn about little Zoë.

I think that as soon as we get to the hotel I will text Sean. It will be okay to do it, right? Shit, what do I do?

* * *

It's only been a few days and I already know I want to live in Montreal one day. It's amazing.

My brother and I have time for ourselves and we also have some quality time with Dad. Well, quality time with Dad means doing insect/nature-related stuff and not talking all that much, but it doesn't matter. Jeremy and I do all the talking. He just looks at us and smiles from time to time. He even takes pictures of the three of us.

Tomorrow, Dad is dragging us to the Laurentian Mountains—the longest hiking trip in the world. He also wants to visit the Botanical Gardens and the Japanese Gardens. Just to get even, we tell him that before we leave, he has to take us to La Ronde, which is kind of a Canadian amusement park.

"The week is going so fast," I say.

"Yeah," Jeremy adds. "I will actually miss you both when you leave."

"I'm hungry. We should get some pasta in that Italian place." Things do not change. Dad is still in his own world. Here we are opening our hearts and he's only thinking about food.

We walk in at Il Campari, Montreal's best. Jeremy says he's never been here before because it's out of his budget. Dad tells him this time this is part of the budget. We take a table, order drinks, and then Dad opens up.

"There's something you boys need to know about Mom," he says.

I can't resist myself and I say, "She isn't our mother?"

Jeremy laughs and adds, "We're adopted?"

I take it further and say, "She's under a spell and that's why she such a mean bitch?"

"Shut up, you two," Dad says. He's trying to be serious, but he's trying to hide something that can be read as a smile. Then he says, "I know Mom has been hard on both of you."

"To *all* of us, you mean," Jeremy adds.

"Yup, to all of us, including our pets," I say.

Dad nods. He takes a sip of his wine and then,

"Well, yes, Mom has been hard to handle for all of us. But there's a reason, and I should have talked to you about this long ago, but I just didn't. It's hard to explain why. Saying it makes it more real, I guess."

Jeremy and I look at each other, and then Jeremy says, "We sorta know, Dad."

"What do you mean?"

"Well, Uncle Robert, he told me all about Mom being bipolar."

"He did? He talked to both of you?" Dad asks.

"Just me. I knew."

"Oh, well . . . I guess this makes it easier. Yes, Mom is bipolar. I guess you both know what that means. And well, even though she's always taken meds, lately things seem to have worsened. She needs help, but you know her, she's too stubborn."

"Wait, so Mom is crazy?" I ask. "And she's going crazier?"

Jeremy hits me on the shoulder. "Shut up, Tom. Dad, how serious is it?"

"Very. Now I feel bad for just leaving her like that. I asked Robert to watch her these days. I hope she hasn't killed him by now."

Like a selfish bastard, I go, "Enough about Mom. Tell me, Dad. Am I bipolar too? Did I inherit Mom's disease, is that why . . . "

But before I can finish my sentence, Jeremy says, "No, Tom, I told you, you're just a plain old pain in the ass." I can't even get mad; my brother is just trying to make things go easy.

Dad then says, "Well, to tell you the truth, it was indeed our concern. But Dr. Stevens explained to us you were not bipolar, you were only suffering depression and anxiety."

So it's for reals, Mom *is* bipolar. That explains a lot, but not all. *Are bipolar people incapable of loving?* I wonder, but decide not to ask.

We order our food and talk about this and that. It's a totally new situation. Dad, Jeremy, and me, just having a nice time. Dad seems to be happy to be with us. Dad shows his love in every one of his smiles.

The best lesson of love I have learned comes from Dad. I can see now that he has been putting up with Mom for so many years; he has been the one trying to make things easier for us. He's been trying to keep his family safe. Just like he does with his insects. He keeps them safe. His ant farm was probably the family he wished he had.

Dad's lesson of love makes me think of Sean. How I want to tell him all this: about Mom, Dad, about Jeremy, and this wonderful trip. I just wanna break the rule I made before flying here and turn on my phone. Yes, I want to. I just want to talk to him.

I search for my phone in my pockets. Fuck. I left it at the hotel. I'll have to wait. I'll do it tonight. I will text him again. Hell, I will even try to call him. Who knows? Maybe since he hasn't heard from me, this time he will pick up, and he will say, "Hey, Tommy."

* * *

Sean did not take my call. My screen is still a monologue. Sean is still mad. I have no clue how I will solve this fucking mess I got us into, but I know I will. I must.

These days in Montreal have taught me so many things. Things about my family, yes, but especially about me. I have learned that my main problem is not that I thought I was a failure, but that I thought everyone else was. Mom, Dad, my brother, my friends. Failures, all of them. That's what I thought.

I see things differently now. I know more about myself. I feel fresh. I feel new. I feel ready to grow up.

We are taking a night flight later today so I decide to give Jeremy and Dad some time on their own and go swim at the hotel's pool. I have so much on my mind! Swimming will help me sort things out.

As soon as I jump in, I start "writing" Sean a letter:

Dear Sean,

I know I'm the last person you wanna talk to. I don't blame you. I don't even blame you for kicking my ass and calling me names with your friends at school. I deserved all that. And more.

Sean, I love you. And I know you love me. What we had was wonderful and I did what I have always managed to do: fuck it all up. I will not try to explain myself; there's really no fucking excuse for what I did. It's just that being with you that weekend made me realize how much I wanted us to be together, to openly be together.

Yes, talking to Lyla was a horrible mistake.

I have been in Montreal with Dad and my brother. I have finally understood what is going on with my mother and what is going on with me . . .

All of a sudden I feel someone pulling me by my

feet. It's Jeremy. He and Dad decided to join me here. I stop writing. I will have time to do it during our flight back home, because now . . . now it is family time.

* * *

I ended up sleeping during the whole flight. No letter for Sean. I will do it once I'm home. Hell, I might even just go to his house and talk to him.

Uncle Robert picks us up at the airport. He seems aloof. He asks about our trip, but before we get to say anything he says, "Tom, I have sad news. Your friend, Sean . . . "

I can't believe it. I can't believe it. This isn't happening. This can't be happening.

As soon as we get home I call Mary. She tells me all about it. Riverside is mourning the death of young Sean Donovan.

"He drove himself to death, Tom," Mary tells me.

"What do you mean?" I ask.

"Well, one minute he is speeding, next minute he's dead."

"How did this happen? I don't understand. He's always been such a responsible driver."

"I don't know. I don't even know if it was an accident or . . . "

"Or what, Mary? OR WHAT?"

"Oh God, listen to me. I don't even know what I'm talking about. Of course, it was an accident. It must have been."

Was it?

Coming back from Montreal is like coming back to a whole new reality. And in this reality, Sean is gone.

CHAPTER TEN
hello, my name is tom

"AREN'T YOU GOING TO SCHOOL?" MOM ASKS me.

"There's no school today," I say without looking at her.

"How come? Oh, is it because of that kid who died? Come on, school can't stop everyone else's lives just because someone died."

"You wouldn't understand," I tell her.

"What I understand is that there's no way I'm going to work and you are staying in bed. Get up, unpack, clean your room, and do the kitchen."

Mom is being Mom. She leaves my room.

I refuse to leave my bed. I didn't sleep at all. I

spent the night reading what everyone posted about Sean's accident. It's stupid how people react. Sean dies and people from school keep posting shit on his wall, as if he was going to read it. He's gone.

Mary texts me and tells me she and Ron are on their way over. They're worried.

* * *

"Everyone thinks this is my fault," I tell them. "Have you read everything people have been posting on Facebook? I don't mean what they wrote on his wall, but what they have written everywhere else."

"You can't pay attention to what people say," Mary says as she runs her fingers through my hair.

"But they are right, Mary. This is all my fault," I say.

"Why? You weren't even here when it happened."

"No, but still, it's my fault. If I hadn't opened my mouth . . . "

"It was an accident," says Ron, "Sean was probably distracted, not for what happened between you two, but . . . I mean, in the end, he lost you, too."

"But he didn't, I . . . "

"You don't have to explain yourself, Tom . . . "

"What time is the service?" I ask.

"At noon, I think. Wait—you're not thinking about going, Tom, are you? That would be a bad idea," Mary says.

"The worst idea," Ron adds. "Besides, you don't have to go."

I don't have to go, I know. But I want to go. I have to.

"I'm going, period. So you can either go with me or leave me alone," I say as I stand up. Mary and Ron look at each other. Neither of them seems to know what to say. I open my closet and start looking for what to wear, because I'm going. Yes, I am.

* * *

As we walk in the church, I see his parents right away. They see me, too. It breaks them to see me. They give me the saddest smiles I've ever seen. I thought they would be mad. I dunno, I thought by this time they would know everything about Sean and me.

Sean's mom opens her arms to me. If she knew, would she do this? Of course not.

"You're here, Tom. Thank you," she says as she hugs me. A short cold hug. Maybe she does know. Maybe they both know and they pretend not to because they are such good Christians.

"Sometimes God's will is so hard to understand." *God's will*, that's what she said. She hugs me again; it feels different this time, warmer. She breaks down and cries. During this time his dad stands right next to us. He's keeping himself together, but you can see that he too thinks this was all God's will.

Then Sean's dad walks me to Sean's coffin. It is closed. He puts his hand on my shoulder and says, "Be with your friend," and he leaves me there. My friend. I place my hand on top of the casket. In my mind, I apologize. I keep repeating, "I'm sorry, Sean. I'm sorry." I try to do my best to keep it together, too, but can't. I just can't. Then I hear some whispering. Hanna's friends.

"What the fuck is he doing here?"

There's a line of people waiting for their turn to say goodbye to Sean. So I walk off and sit down on one of the benches between Mary and Ron. They are crying and I know they are not crying for him, because they really didn't know him. They are crying for me, with me.

It is then that Hanna decides to come to us and says, "Tom, you should leave. Leave now."

She wants me out. She looks both sad and mad. She's crying. She feels as bad as I do.

"He has a right to be here," Mary says.

"I think your friend has done enough already," Hanna says. "He has no right to be here. Did you hear me, Tom?" Hanna keeps whispering things to me, but I don't understand. I know she isn't using the F word to address me. She doesn't need to.

It's like she has created this whole new language in which the words stab me slowly, painfully.

I stand up. Ron and Mary stand up too. Before we walk out of the chapel, I stand for a minute and then take one last look to Sean's coffin. I lose it. I can't help myself and I cry, I cry so loud that everybody turns to look at me.

I fall on my knees and start to slap my face. Mary or Ron—I don't know who—grabs me. They do their best to calm me down but I just keep slapping my face.

"Stop, Tom, stop."

"Breathe, Tom, breathe!"

I just can't. This isn't happening. Sean cannot be dead.

No.

* * *

Ron drives and Mary sits in the backseat with me. We say nothing. We stay quiet all the way to my house. When Ron parks, none of us move. We stay in our seats, minutes feel like hours. It's like we've always been here in this car carrying this feeling.

Mary finally breaks the silence and says, "Hey, let's get you home. You should go to bed and rest."

Ron comes out of the car and opens the door for me. Mary helps me out. They walk by my side. I tell them I will be okay and I continue on my own. I don't even say goodbye. I don't even thank them.

Before I even try to get my keys, Dad opens the door. He pulls me into his arms. He asks, "Where were you, Tom? I was worried." I can't control myself. I start crying again. I feel it—I feel it all over my skin, pain. Horrible pain. Sharp breath-taking pain.

"I can't, Dad. I can't anymore. Take me to Dr. Stevens. Take me to the clinic. Take me out of here." And I start all over again. I beat my head. I slap my face.

"Stop. Stop it, Tom," he says, trying to restrain my hands.

Mom gets home right at that moment. She starts yelling, "What is it? What is going on here?" She's disoriented. It's like she realizes this is not her son throwing another tantrum. This is not her son picking a fight. This is not her son threatening to kill himself.

This is her son surrendering.

"Tommy? Tommy, what's happening?" she says.

I feel like a child in her arms. I feel like the sick child she once took care of.

* * *

During the whole ride Dad tries to convince me not to go.

"Stay home, we'll help you."

I want to say, *It takes more than good intentions to help a son.* I want to say, *Dad, I am gay and I just lost my boyfriend. Can you understand that?* But I can't. Something has changed within me. I don't feel like fighting back.

"Are you sure this is what you want?" Dad asks me.

"I am. I don't expect you to understand it, Dad. It's just, it's just that I feel lost."

"It's so sad, this thing with Sean." My dad's words feel cold, just as cold as the newspaper story: "*Star of the swim team of Riverside High School, killed in a car accident on Scenic Road . . .*"

"It's not sad, Dad, it's a tragedy, at least for me because Sean . . . " I'm about to tell him. I think I want to explain it to him. I'm sick of the secrecy, but Dad interrupts me.

"You don't have to tell me anything you are not ready to share. I understand, I understand perfectly, or, at least, I try."

I do not know what to say.

He continues, "I just wish you didn't have to go to this place to sort things out. I wish we were enough . . . I wish *I* was enough for you. I know I haven't been there for you all that much."

"In a way, you have."

"No, Thomas. I haven't. I haven't been there

for you and your brother. Your mom's situation has taken all of my time. Believe me, having Jeremy in Montreal is not all right. It's like helping him run away instead of learning how to deal with . . . "

"Mom."

"Yes."

I feel again the need to say something. Part of me wants to say, *But you haven't done so and you will never be able to because you're a fucking pussy.* Part of me wants to say, *Don't worry, Dad, I understand.* It would have been a lie, though.

The road to the teen mental clinic is beautiful. The tallest, greenest pines you have ever seen guard it. I'm not sure I noticed them when I first came in a year ago or when I left. I stay silent the whole way, tears running down my cheeks.

When we get to the gate, Dad stops. He looks at me, his eyes asking me one more time, *Are you sure?*

I look at the sign on my right.

RIVERSIDE TEEN MENTAL CLINIC
Providing quality medical and mental health care for Riverside County children and teens since 1995.

I turn to Dad, answering with my own eyes, *Yes, Dad, I'm sure.* Dad drives through the gate. I can see he's sad. I can see this isn't what he wanted for me. I can see there are too many things he wants to say but can't. He just can't.

I get out of the car. Dad opens the trunk, hands me my suitcase and for the first time in many years, I say, "I love you, Dad."

Any dad would have embraced his son after such words. Dad isn't like any dad, we know that. But I see something different in him, like he's about to break. He does his best by saying, "Take care, son."

He's heading to the driver's side of the car when I stop him. "You actually have to come inside with me and sign my admission, remember?" He looks surprised; he even makes a joke, "What if I don't? What if we run away together?"

"Again?" I say.

"When have we . . . ?"

"Remember Montreal, Dad?"

"It seems so long ago."

Dad signs papers. I sign papers. They check my stuff. No phones, no iPods, no razors, no lotions. Check, check, check. A nurse and a doctor receive me and promise they will take care of me. I say goodbye.

Dad says, "See you soon."

It's only now that I realize Dr. Stevens isn't around. I thought he would be. I wanted to see him. Seeing him will feel like a step towards recovery, although coming here feels like a step back.

I feel like sinking and swimming at the same time.

"Ready, Thomas?" says the nurse, "I'll walk you in. You will be sharing a room with Billy. He will either amuse you or amaze you."

"You're telling me *you* are Tom, one of the Misfits?" Billy asks.

"Yup."

"I don't believe you!"

"Why? Do I look too normal?"

"No, I mean, yes. It's just that . . . " Billy pauses. "I dunno, I pictured all of you way older."

"How come?"

"I don't know, maybe 'cause you were *the* Misfits."

"You didn't think we were the *actual* Misfits, did you?"

"Ehm, no, no, of course not."

"Anyway," I continue, "if we're going to share this room, we have to set things straight."

"Hey, how come *you* get to set the rules?" Billy asked. "I was here first."

"Didn't you pay attention to my story? *I* was here first."

"You mean you've been grandfathered in or something?"

"I guess you could say that."

Billy stares at me. "You're a butthead, you know that?"

"Believe me, I do . . . Anyway, why are *you* here?"

"Wow, you finally ask. I thought you didn't care."

"Why?"

"Because you spent the last million hours talking about yourself."

"Hey, you *asked* me why I was here," I retort.

"Yes, but you're *so* self-centered," Billy replied. "Hasn't anyone ever told you that?"

"Yeah," I laugh, "but I tell them to fuck off."

"Wow, how elegant! You're the family stone, eh?"

"More like the ugly duckling, Mom would say."

"OMG, an almost-swan is sharing room with me. What a blessing."

"Jesus, don't you ever keep thoughts to yourself?"

"Never."

"Me neither. I guess we have something in common," I observed.

Billy just looks at me. "And?"

"And . . . ?" I wait for him to make his point.

Billy continues, "Lemme rephrase it for you: 'I didn't realize that I spent hours talking about me without asking about you, dear Billy Jean.'"

"'Billy Jean,' is that your name?"

"It is."

"Like that old Michael Jackson song?"

"Yup."

"Well, Billy Jean, you could have left. You could have said something."

"Could I? You wanted me to go and play Scrabble at the Lounge? You wanted me to go and watch another episode of *Parenthood*? No way. At least your story was interesting."

"You're definitely a butthead, too, Billy. So, are you going to tell me your story or not?"

"I don't eat," he replies.

"What?"

"Yeah, I don't eat. That's why I'm here."

"Isn't that more of a girl issue?"

"Oh, yeah, that too."

"What do you mean?"

"That's part of my story, too. I have a girl issue. I wanna be a girl."

"Oh, you're gay?"

"Gay? No motherfucking way, no. A girl, I wanna be a girl."

"Oh."

"Yeah, oh."

I've been lying on my bed, talking and talking since I set foot in this room. I've been talking for "a million hours," according to my roommate without even caring who he is. Now I'm curious, I sit up straight and take a good look at Billy Jean. His hair, his clothing, all of him looks like he's gift-wrapped. He's skinny and taller than me. He's fourteen, or maybe fifteen. His blonde wavy hair makes me think of a girl who is too young to comb it herself. Messy but pretty at the same time, as if she had just woken up. I mean, as if *he* had just woken up.

Billy brings me back to the conversation. "Maybe that's why he put us together."

"Who?"

"Dr. Stevens, duh!"

"Yeah, maybe. Do you see him?" I ask.

"I have seen him, but he isn't my therapist if that's what you're asking."

"Oh."

"I don't think he's seeing patients now."

"He isn't?"

"Nope. I heard he comes and goes because he's teaching a seminar, or taking a seminar, I don't know. We all meet with the younger doctors and go to group therapy. He sometimes comes to the group sessions, but he just sits down and takes notes, like he's the nerdiest student in your class."

"I wonder if he will make an exception with me. I was looking forward to seeing him."

"Why, because you are special? Dude, you are

just like all of us. If we don't see him, you don't see him, period."

Billy is right. That's the one thing I have learned in the last few weeks. I'm no exception. I'm just as fucked up as everybody else in this world. I'm just another insect on the ground.

"Kids, time for your pills."

The nurse hands Billy Jean three pills. I get two.

"Will I get sleepy?" I ask.

"No. Not with these."

"They save the sleepy-time ones for later," explains Billy Jean as he swallows his without water. The nurse gives him an eye, and then leaves the glass of water on our night table.

I lie back on my bed and ask, "So, now that we are done with me, it's your turn to tell me your story, and don't save any details."

"Ha ha, you nosy girl. Where should I start?" Billy Jean makes room on my bed for himself, lies down next to me and says, "My real name is William but nobody ever calls me that . . . "

* * *

I'm asked to start, so I go, "Hello, my name is Tom."

"Hello, To—"

"Do we really have to start like this everyday? I mean, we all know our names by now, don't we?" I say.

"It's the rules, Tom, you know that," Norma, our therapist, says.

"Besides, you don't know everybody's names, do you?" says Billy Jean. I ignore him.

"Fine. Hello, everybody. My name is Tom."

"Hello, Tom."

Norma then asks me to share something I have learned this week.

"This week I have realized that mornings are great, I mean, maybe not great, more like okay, but nights, nights are hell."

"Tell us about it."

It's weird to be in this group. This group without

them, my friends, my Misfits. I see them, though. I see Julie in the eyes of that girl with the flowery Converse. I see Harry in that kid who is checking out this other girl's legs. I don't see Sarah yet, but I know she's here, too. I wonder if Sarah is Billy Jean.

"Well, when I wake up, I'm okay. I don't feel or think or anything."

"The beauty of meds," a kid says. What's his name?

"Yeah, I guess," I reply. "The thing is that in the morning, I feel like I am okay, like nothing too bad has happened. I take a shower, get breakfast, and go to the reading room and everything is fine."

"What are you reading?" Norma asks.

"*It's Kind of a Funny Story.*"

"Why?" She asks.

"Why what?" I ask her back.

"Why is it kind of a funny story?" she says.

"That's the title of the book."

"What is it about?" someone else asks.

"It's about this kid who is as fucked up as we all are," I say.

"I read it. I liked it, I liked it better than . . . " someone else adds.

"Is this a freaking book club or what?" says Billy Jean, being the bitch I know now he can be.

"Calm down, everybody," Norma says, "So, Tom, you were telling us . . . "

I have such a weird feeling. I feel like shit but I still find all this funny. I like the interruptions. I like how we are all over the place in our conversations.

"What I wanted to explain is that in the mornings everything seems normal. It's like I'm not thinking clearly of why I am here. But after dinner I always feel like shit."

"Maybe you need to take a shit?" Billy Jean says without even looking at me. I ignore him and continue.

"I can't stop crying and I have this urge, this big fat urge to yell, to run, to hit my face. The worst thing is the crying. I can't stop. I can't sleep, and when I do, all I dream is about Sean."

"He does cry a lot, I must say. I'm this close

to asking the nurse to double my doses so I can actually sleep," says Billy Jean.

I want to let it go, but I can't. "Shut up, asshole." My hands start shaking, my heart's beating fast and I feel it. I know it's coming, I start crying.

I turn to Billy and I read a subtle, "I'm sorry," from his lips.

"Isn't group therapy supposed to make us feel better, Norma?" I ask. But before she says something I hear *his* voice.

"Group therapy is not only about feeling better. That's temporary. Group therapy is about healing and sometimes the only way to heal is to visit the darkest moments." Dr. Stevens. How long has he been here? I wanna run and hug him. I feel like a kid that has just seen Santa. Of course, I refrain.

"But that's why we're here, right? To be away from our darkest moments," some girl says. God, I don't know anybody's name.

"No, you are here to *take away* those darkest

moments and the only way to do so is by acknowledging them," Dr. Stevens states.

"Now, Tom, tell us, why do you think you want to beat yourself?" Norma asks me.

"I dunno," I reply.

I really don't know. I think of what Jeremy and I talked about back in Montreal. I think of all those episodes when I tried to hurt myself, those episodes that I had forgotten about. I say, "I just wanna."

"And do you? Do you hurt yourself?"

"Yes. Sometimes."

"And how does that make you feel?"

Billy Jean looks at me and starts laughing. He repeats, *"And how does that make you feel, Thomas?"* I can't help myself and I laugh too. Nobody seems to understand what's going on with us, but they all start laughing too.

Dr. Stevens gets it. He sees what he has done. All those sessions with the Misfits come back to him. "All right, all right, we all needed a good laugh, right? So any ideas of why Tom wants to hurt himself?"

His question kills my laugh. I think about it. I ask myself, *How do I feel after slapping myself or hitting myself on the head?*

"To punish himself," says Billy Jean.

"To feel something else," says the girl who looks like Julie.

"What do you mean I wanna feel something else?" I ask.

"Something else, something that's not your own mourning. Something besides that guilt that you carry around everywhere. How do you feel afterwards?" the same girl adds.

"I feel . . . I feel . . . I feel relieved, actually."

"Finally someone gets it. Relieved. That's the word. That's how I feel every time I throw up," says Billy Jean. "I mean, every time I *threw* up because I haven't done it in a while now. Promise. Girl Scout's honor," he says, trying to make us laugh, only this time no one laughs. We are all serious, looking at each other. We are all here because we have dangerous ways to feel relieved.

Norma tells me that I should try to distract myself every time I feel like hurting myself.

"How?" I ask.

She then addresses the whole group and says, "Any ideas, guys? Just remember the only condition is that your relief is not a threat to you or anyone around you."

"I heard throwing ice cubes at a wall feels just as great as breaking glasses or dishes," says one girl.

"I guess drawing, painting, or writing can also help."

More kids share or invent ideas to help us in those moments of crisis. I just hear them. I hear each one of those crazy ideas. Norma must have noticed I was there but not there because she asks me, "What do you think, Tom? Do you think you could adopt any of these strategies?"

I look at her. I want to say, *Yes, sure*, but I would

be lying, and if there's something I have learned in these last two weeks, it is that lying makes things worse.

"But how do you push yourself to do something like that when all you want is to sit down and cry your soul out? How do you convince yourself not to beat yourself up for all the damage you've . . . ?" I can't even finish my sentence. I start crying again. Everyone looks at me. I see two or three of the girls around me eye-tearing, too.

"You just do it," says Billy Jean. "You just grow some balls and do it because the pain inside is more than enough. You don't need pain outside yourself, too."

There's an air of peace after these words. Billy's the youngest in the room and yet he's the wisest. He really is growing on me. He was right; it makes sense that we're roommates.

* * *

I sorta lost it. It was almost the end of my second week here. I was trying to release my pain by writing a letter to Sean. Next thing I know I'm striking through all my words and when there was no more space on the paper I started on my hand, my arm. I went insane.

So they have changed my doses. I now get four pills throughout the day. One in the morning. One after lunch and two after dinner. I know I'm taking Zoloft, but I really don't know what else they are giving me. They are also keeping me under watch; I guess Norma and Dr. Stevens have advised the staff that I might hurt myself. But I haven't done it in two or three days, maybe more. You really lose track of time here.

I miss Mary. I miss Ron. But mostly, I miss Sean.

* * *

Group therapy is cool. Yesterday it was Billy Jean's turn to read about his childhood. Norma, our therapist, is making us write. Hearing everyone's story, I felt embarrassed about my shit. I mean, about Mom's shit. Yes, she shoved us around our whole lives, but that seems harmless compared to what some people have experienced. One of the girls' stepdads, for example, used to do stuff to her and her mom always knew about it and never did shit. I know this doesn't actually explain why group therapy is cool. It's just that it makes you realize that people have dark places—darker than yours.

Tomorrow is visiting weekend. Dad said he and Uncle Robert would come. It seems they are hanging out a lot more now. I like Uncle Robert. He's easygoing compared to Dad. He probably thinks the same about Jeremy and me; Jeremy being the easygoing one of course. I wonder if Mom will come and visit.

Jeremy emailed me yesterday. He says that I have to get better so that I can be ready for my "fucking amazing summer in Montreal." Thank God, they changed the rules now and we can check our emails a couple of times a week. Not Facebook, though. As Billy Jean says, "Facebook is the devil."

Oh, and the weirdest thing happened this week. I got an email from Charlie Dale. I was like, *What the fuck?* I didn't dare read it. Everyone at St. Mary's probably knows my whole story and how I ended up here *again*. I don't need that shit, I don't.

* * *

It's been almost a month, a month! Things are not as shitty, or so it seems. Of course, I think of Sean all the time, but I don't cry anymore. I mean, I don't *always* cry. Just at nights, as soon as the lights are off, I see it coming. It's like a punch. Sometimes Billy Jean pretends not to hear me. Other times he stands up and sits next to me. He holds my hand not saying a word. He's just there. He had a relapse yesterday and things got messy. It was my turn to take care of him. Him crying, me holding his hand, some cleaning lady mopping the floor, cleaning his mess.

Hanging out with Billy Jean helps. It's like we take turns feeling like shit. He says we should make sure not to be shitty the same day because no one would be there for us, holding our hands. "Well, maybe the cleaning lady would," he says. He makes me laugh all the fucking time.

There's this dude—the one who looks like Harry—his name is Jimmy; well, Jimmy messes around with us all the time. He says Billy Jean is my girlfriend. Billy Jean says, "As if!" That's his catchphrase. I told him it was a very 90s thing to say—Billy Jean has this obsession with the 90s. Anyway, Billy Jean adds, "You're more my type, Jimmy. If only you didn't smell like rotten vegetables." I applaud Billy's moves.

Jimmy goes, "Fuck off."

End of story.

"You know I don't like you *that* way, right?" Billy Jean tells me when this happens.

"I know, I know," I tell him.

"You're too chubby." He's probably right. The

last couple of weeks I have been eating like a pig, even though the food here isn't that great—it's hospital food. I used to train more than four times a week and now I don't do shit. We are allowed to use the swimming pool. We even have a lifeguard. It's rather small—the pool, I mean—while the life-guard is huge. Still, I don't dare swim.

Not yet.

* * *

I tell Billy Jean about Charlie Dale. He had his own Charlie Dale episode. His was messier. Also, Billy was actually in love with his Charlie Dale and he not only wrote him about his feelings, he even had the balls to go and say, "I love you." His Charlie Dale punched him in the face and Billy punched back. He broke the other kid's nose.

"So, have you opened that fucking email?" he says as he walks to the reading room.

"What?" I know he's talking about Charlie Dale's email but I pretend not to understand shit.

"You know, *the* email. Charlie Dale's."

"No."

"I can do it for you."

"Are you seriously saying that, again?"

"Bitch, I can read it for you. If it is too bad, I will delete it and erase it from my mind."

"And if it isn't too bad?"

"Then I memorize it for you, duh."

Billy Jean is a real Misfit and—considering how skinny he is and how fat I am—he's more of a Miss Fit than I am. I have to tell him that one of these days—he would love it. I think of my Misfits: Harry, Julie, and Sarah. Dr. Stevens never asks about any of them. I mean, not that he has to, but we were an item, him included.

God, isn't this sad? The best times of my life are always in this place.

CHAPTER ELEVEN
time to go

"So," Dad says.

"So," I tell him.

Silence. Silence.

"You two really can't communicate, can you?" says Uncle Robert. He's losing his patience with Dad and me. He adds, "How have you been feeling, Tom? You ready to leave this place?"

"Okay. And no."

"You look well, though," says Dad.

"More than well. Looks they're feeding you all right." My uncle pats my cheek. I know he means I've been putting on some weight. I have. I look chubby. That's what happens when you eat half of

Billy Jean's plates so he doesn't get in trouble. But I don't say any of that.

Instead, I say, "Yeah, food here is five stars. We have a French chef and shit." As soon as I say it, I feel sick. What's the point of bitching, really?

"Wow, you are definitely better, you recovered your—" Uncle Robert starts saying.

"Humor," ends Dad.

Fuck. They drove here just to see me and I have already started off on the wrong foot. But they laugh and Dad adds, "Robert, maybe we should move in here."

"Yes, we should, I fancy having crepes every morning . . . "

We all laugh at my uncle's fake French accent.

Then I say, "I'm sorry, I didn't mean to be rude or anything. It's just that, I've been gaining weight. It's not like I don't notice it. It's just . . . "

"Are you not training?" asks Dad.

"No."

"You should. Swimming always makes you feel better," Dad tells me. "It even makes you happy."

"It's what happens to your dad when he's with his insects—makes him happy," Uncle Robert jokes.

I see Dad and Uncle Robert and I see two adults and at the same time I see two kids. I see Jeremy and me. I see how different they are and how similar they are to us. I always thought Jeremy was more like Dad, and now . . . now, I don't really know. They keep arguing about shit, and for a second I see them like those grumpy old men from the Muppets. It's funny. I can't help but laugh at them.

We spend the afternoon talking. I tell them about Billy Jean, about group therapy, and about the classes we take. They seem surprised about the classes we get here.

"Man, I should stay here with you. I could use some classes like yours."

Uncle Robert has always been sort of curious about technology and shit. He keeps asking me question about my App and Communication Class.

"If you create an App, maybe you can sell it to people and get tons of money?"

"That's not how it works, Robert," Dad says. "You have to sell it to a bigger company and . . . "

"Time to say goodbye, kids," one of the nurses says.

It was sad seeing them leave. I had never felt that way about my family before. As I was waving goodbye, I imagined me with them in the car, me and Jeremy. I imagined all of us going on a road trip: the kind of road trip that we went on when we were kids—that I hated. I would hate it now, too, but it would be a different hate. I cry and cry but don't feel like hurting myself or anything. It feels good to cry like this, for them.

* * *

"Tom,

I hope you are OK. I heard you were back at the Clinic (in case you are wondering, Emily told my sister and my sister told me)."

"Who is Emily?" asks Billy, interrupting his own reading.

"I told you about her. She was my brother's girl-friend."

"Oh, the one who he was banging."

"Yeah, that one."

"I know I should have written this letter long, long ago. I should have done it last year, when you ended up there. I felt bad about it. I kept thinking, *Tom is there because of me*, which is probably the way you feel about your friend Sean."

Billy Jean is reading me Charlie's email. He read the first paragraph on his own, then decided to print it because, "No way I could memorize all that shit," he says.

When you left, and all that shit happened,

I was sent to counseling, more because of my rage outbreak than anything. I thought, *This is gonna suck ass.* I mean you remember Mr. Lang and how boring he is. And it didn't suck ass, but then he sent me with some-one else. A psichotherapyst or something. Anywey, with her I opened up and I went from feeling fucking mad at you, to feeling super guilty, to learning about it. She told me that I would have reacted the same way if you had banged my sister (she didn't use that word) or a girlfriend of mine. She said that I reacted the way I did because I felt betreyed.

"OMG, this guy killed the spelling bee!"
"Shut up, keep reading."

I know you meant well in that letter but by writing it, by opening up with so many feelings,? you took away something from me, my friend. You. Things weren't going to be the same.

Fuck, who is the cheesy one now? (joke).

"Ha ha."

I am not trying to say, "hey, I did what I did because you deserved it." Not at all. But mine was a <u>reaction</u>. A stupid one, but a reaction, period. It was you who decided to kill yourself, as a reaction. I did not push it (although I am sure I did not help), it was your decision. I learned to see it that way. I know I never looked for you or anything, but I want you to forgive me, I overreacted and because of that well . . . you know.

What I am saying is, and I feel way more intelligent than I actually am (and you know I am not smart at all).

"And now *I* know that."

"Goddamnit, Billy, keep reading."

Now that everybody is saying that it was no accident, that Sean Donovan did kill himself, well, his was a reaction. That was his own way of handling things. Just like you did. Difference is, he did kill himself and you didn't and I am glad you didn't. I can't ask anything but I can tell you that I miss my friend. Now who is gay? (joke).
Take care,
C.D.

Fucking hell, my parents are spending a whole lot of money to have me here and in the end it becomes more helpful to read an email from Charlie than going to group therapy.

"Well, he might not know how to spell but he sure can write, right?" I say, and Billy Jean laughs his ass off until he realizes I'm crying. I don't even know why.

Charlie was my best friend. We were together at St. Mary's since kindergarten . . . Didn't become friends until way later, but once we did, we would always hang out. Whenever things with my mom got rough, Charlie was there for me. He used to say, "All moms are nuts. Yours might be nuttier, but, oh well." Then he found us something to do: We'd have long Halo tournaments. I didn't like video games all that much, but it was better than feeling like shit.

We got in trouble so many times—*so* many times. And we had such great times—*such* great times. I hated him because I thought he had shown my letter to everybody. I hated him for hurting me so much, for not understanding. I wasn't even in love with him, or, at least, that's not what my letter was about. Mine was a loving letter not a love letter. But now, hating is so not important to me. Plus, if I ended up in here, it's because I decided it. Me, not my parents, or my teachers, or anyone. Me. I did this to me.

"So, you think Charlie Dale is gay after all?" Billy Jean asks me.

"Ha ha. Nah, he isn't," I say.

"You sure?"

"No, but, does it matter?"

"It does if he's cute. Is he cute?"

"Kinda."

"Are you going to write back?"

"I don't know."

"If you don't, I will," Billy Jean says.

* * *

It's been seven weeks since I arrived. I haven't cried or hurt myself for the past nine days. I tell everyone in group therapy and Billy Jean says, "Wow, Norma, you getting him the gold star of sanity to stick on his forehead?"

"Bitch," I tell him.

"But so beautiful," he states.

"Kids, kids, come on," Norma says, "I'm happy

for you, Thomas. We all are, aren't we?" I see some of the kids couldn't care less. A few of them smile, they share my happiness.

"It's a small step, I know," I say.

"A step is a step," one girl says.

"Ay, enough about him," Billy Jean yells. "It's my turn now."

Norma looks at me and asks me with her eyes if I'm okay with changing the subject. I nod. She then asks Billy Jean if he has something new to share.

"Oh, do I!? Check this out, y'all. I dreamt I was a cupcake!" We all start to laugh, even Norma. "Shut up, I *am* serious, and let me tell you I wasn't just any cupcake. No, sir, I was a chocolate cream-filled vanilla cupcake with, hear this, raspberry-chipotle frosting."

"Come on, Billy, be serious," one boy says.

"I *am* serious. I swear, that's what I dreamt."

"Norma, please, tell him something," someone says.

Norma's laughter goes from hard to subtle. She clears her throat. "Let's all say it did happen. Let's say Billy did dream he was a . . . what was it?"

"A chocolate cream-filled vanilla cupcake with raspberry-chipotle frosting."

"Okay, that." Then she asks us, "What do you think that means?"

We all start to speculate and come up with statements like:

1. Billy is happy to be gay.
2. Billy is hungry.
3. Billy is pregnant.
4. Billy is sweet and spicy at the same time. (His favorite idea.)
5. Billy is lost.

I don't know how Norma does it, but she takes us from a Technicolor cupcake discussion to a more existential topic: *How do you want to see yourself in the future?*

When we finished our session, I asked Billy Jean that question again, and he answered, "Like a way-improved version of Lady Gaga, of course."

* * *

My birthday is tomorrow. I will be seventeen. I overhear Billy Jean outside our room. He's telling one of the girls that we all need a party. He also confesses to her that he's planning a surprise party for me at the pool. He says he has managed already to get us a cake. A double-chocolate cake that he might not even eat.

I hear him opening the door and I pretend to be sleeping. I don't wanna ruin this for him, he sounded so excited a while ago. I think he's right, we all need a party.

"Thomas?" the nurse calls me. I keep my eyes closed.

"Thomas?" she repeats.

"Tom-Tom, Nurse Jackie is calling you," says Billy Jean.

I hear the nurse say, "I told you not to call me that. I hate that show, she's a junkie," says the nurse. "Thomas, you have a phone call."

I open my eyes and ask, "Who is it, my father?"

"No, it's your mom. Come pick it up at the nurse's station."

Mom . . . *Mom* is calling me?

* * *

If my life were a movie, the scene of me talking to Mom on the phone yesterday would have been very different. We would probably cry and say *I-love-you*'s to each other. Instead we just performed some sorta interview.

"How are you, Tom?"

"Fine, how're you?"

"I'm okay."

"Good. How's Dad?"

"He's okay."

"Good."

"So . . . "

"So."

But then she started opening up. "We are going to

Chicago tomorrow. I have to see my doctor. I know your father already told you about . . . my *situation*."

"He did."

"We are going to be away for just for a few days."

"Okay."

"So."

"So?"

"Take good care of yourself, please. And . . . "

"And?"

"And if something comes up, please call your Uncle Robert."

"I will."

"I mean, you can contact us, too, of course, but he will be closer to you."

"Noted."

"Okay."

"Okay."

"Hey, Happy Birthday."

"It's tomorrow."

"I know, I just . . . I just wanted to be the first to say it. You be good, okay, Tommy?"

"Will do . . . Mom?"

"Yes?"

"Thank you for calling."

Tommy. My mother called me *Tommy*. *Tommy*, I'm *Tommy* again. I don't know how I feel except that this whole thing feels different.

* * *

The kids here have "tricked" me into coming to the pool. As I enter, I see a big colorful banner that reads, HAPPY B-DAY TOM! It's weird: I don't think I have had a party in years. Everyone takes off their clothes, revealing swimsuits underneath.

They jump in the pool. They yell. They laugh. Especially Billy Jean.

"Come on, Thomas, get in," one of the girl says.

I feel like one of those little boys too afraid of being in the water, and at the same time, so eager to get into it.

"But I have no swimsuit, how will I . . . "

I don't even get to finish my sentence, Billy Jean pushes me inside the pool with my clothes on. My first reaction is to immediately swim back and get out of the water.

"Are you mad?" one of the girls asks.

"No," I said. "I'm . . . I'm just wet."

"Naaauuuughty!" yells Billy Jean as he jumps right in. "Come on, get in. Just go in your boxers, they're decent, I've seen them. No one will say a word, right girls?"

"I prefer to try some of these chips and salsa," I say as I walk to the table.

* * *

We are getting ready for bed. Billy Jean asks me if I'm upset.

"Why?"

"Because you're old now, and because I pushed you into the pool."

"No, not at all."

"Not even a little?"

"No, seriously. I just didn't feel like being in the pool. But everything else was great. Thank you for the party."

"My pleasure."

"Hey, did I see you eating the cake?" I ask him.

"I dunno, did you?"

"I think I did."

"And?"

"Well, it's amazing—you ate!"

"Don't make a big deal out of it, everybody ate from that cake, even though it wasn't chocolate cream-filled vanilla with raspberry-chipotle frosting."

"Ha ha, I know, but . . . "

"No buts, Thomas. If I'm gonna be normal, it gotta seem normal."

I kiss him. But it isn't a love kiss. It is more of a loving kiss. Billy Jean is a great friend. He's the friend I needed. He's like a bolder version of me or something. He is snappy and bitchy and witty and . . . I really enjoy his company. He reminds me of

Michael, Billy Elliot's friend. I will miss him once I get out of here. I mean, the way I see things, I will get out of here sooner than he will.

I'm glad Billy Jean is eating. One, because it means he's getting better and, two, well, because I don't have to help him anymore. Last week it was forbidden to sit next to him during our meals. One of the nurses would sit across from him at the table and wouldn't move until Billy was done.

When he told me he had an eating disorder, I imagined he was one of those kids who eats and then throws up. "That kills your teeth and creates monster breath. I prefer not eating." Sometimes he does. Throw up, I mean. Not too often but when he does, it's a mess. He gets hysterical and cries and yells and throws up and curses everyone. Even me.

Billy was not eating because he didn't want to gain weight. It seems he was chubby when he was a kid and everyone made fun of him. I'm sure people made fun of him because he would always dress himself in his mother's clothes but, hey, what do

I know? I think he's just confused. I mean, he says he wants to be a girl but his hair and his clothes and everything about him is always a mess. He has never asked us to refer to him as her. Isn't that what dudes who wanna be girls do?

I sometimes dressed in my mother's clothes, too, but not once did I think of being a girl. I like being a guy. I like who I am.

Wow, have I ever said that before? *I like who I am.*

* * *

Yesterday, I talked about swimming at group therapy. Everybody believes that swimming would make me happy and that I don't wanna be happy.

I don't know what to think. I actually don't want to think. That is the main reason I would like to try swimming. It's the only place I have ever felt free. When you're swimming, you don't think, you just swim. The only thing on your mind is getting to the other side. That's all I want—to get to the other side, wherever that is.

I have been thinking about Charlie Dale. It started when Billy Jean read me the letter. Sean and Charlie: they are both on my mind. I have always been the one writing letters. I wrote letters to Sean all the time. Charlie's was actually the first letter someone had written to me. I wonder if I should write back. What could I say?

My letters under the water. I had forgotten how much I liked doing that. When I have a letter on my mind, I take it to the pool. I think of what I wanna say. It's like dictating to myself. Maybe I could do that: go swimming and think up a letter to Charlie. I would be solving two issues at once.

"Norma is ready to see you," the nurse tells me. I'm having my one-on-one session with her. I sit on the sofa, right across from her chair. She's wearing some old Converses. They make her look young.

"It was interesting hearing you talk about

swimming yesterday," Norma begins. "Tell me more about that. When did you start?"

"When I was ten. Dad wanted me to do sports and I didn't like any sport. Also I sucked at everything."

"But not swimming?" She asks.

"No," I say.

"And have you decided about swimming here yet?"

"No."

She writes something down. I imagine her writing: Subject likes swimming and is afraid of it.

"I'm not afraid of swimming though."

"Who said anything about you being afraid?"

It seems like today Norma decided to roughen things up. She asks me if I have been in touch with Mom. I tell her she has called me only once.

"Do you think of her?"

"Not really. I'm better off without her."

I'm expecting her to say, "I sense some kind of anger in your words." But Norma only says, "I see."

"I do wonder what she thinks of all this." My own words surprise me. Where did they come from?

"What do you think is on her mind?"

"About me?"

"Yes, and about you being here."

"She probably thinks I'm a fucking pussy that can't deal with his shit on his own."

"And what do you think?"

"About me?"

"Yes."

"That I'm a fucking pussy and can't deal with my shit on my own." As soon as I finish my sentence I realize I have done it again, talked without thinking.

"You seem shocked, Tom. Tell me what is really on your mind right now."

"That it's true. I'm my mother."

* * *

After what has been the most disturbing fucking therapy session, I go to the reading room. One computer is available, so I decide to check my email. Mary has written. She says she misses me. She says she probably doesn't understand what I'm going through but she's willing to try. She says she will be there for me once I get out. Mary. I haven't been a good friend to her. I miss her and Ron and my life before all this happened. My life before Sean. My life with Sean.

I go to my room, grab my swimsuit and my towel, sign the log, and dive into the pool. There are a few kids in the water and the lifeguard is around, cleaning up.

The fucking pool receives me with no regrets. The fucking pool makes me feel fresh and free. The fucking pool makes me wanna move faster and faster and I do. I swim as fast as I can, touch one end and then turn around to the other. Stroke after stroke I think of everything that has happened in the last few weeks, the last few months. It all started in a pool, it all has to end in a pool. I'm thinking about Sean. I talk to him. I tell him I'm sorry. I am sorry about everything. I talk to Jeremy and thank him for telling me all that stuff back in Montreal, teaching me about myself. I talk to Dad and I tell him he has to pay less attention to his insects and more attention to us. Then I do it, for the first time, I do it. I say, "Come on, Thomas. You can do it. You can. Just swim. You can do it. You can get out of all this shit. You can make it. Deal with it. Just learn to deal with it."

Stroke after stroke after stroke. Then everything turns white, then black. I can't breathe. I can't breathe.

* * *

This is how I remember it.

I open my eyes and Sean is there. He is calling me only I can't actually hear him. I can feel his hands on my chest. He pushes one, two, three times. All of a sudden, Sean turns his back and leaves. I want to reach out. I want him not to go. Then I feel like throwing up and I spring up. I puke water. I'm startled. It takes me a second to realize where I am. The sounds become clear now. Billy Jean is there.

He yells, "Fucking asshole, why did you do it? Why did you try to kill yourself?"

"No, he didn't. I saw it all," the lifeguard says. "He was just swimming too fast. Tom, are you okay?

I'm still confused. "Am I alive?" I ask.

"Yes, you asshole. You're talking to us, aren't you?" Billy Jean says.

"I saw Sean," I say.

"Sean? Nah, you're probably confusing him with Mr. Lifeguard right here. I'm going to drown, too, just to feel his lips."

The lifeguard stands up and leaves, not without saying, "Do you want me to call a doctor?"

"No, I'll be fine."

"He'd be better if you do some mouth to mouth," Billy Jean tells the lifeguard who gives him a finger.

I laugh and laugh and laugh.

I stay on the floor for a while, trying to catch my breath. Billy Jean stays by my side.

"Come on, butthead. Get up. We'll miss pizza

night if we don't hurry up. Believe it or not, I'm hungry today."

The rest of the kids who were around me when it all happened have left now. Billy Jean helps me up. I see his arm, he has some kind of red bite.

"What's that on your arm?" I ask him.

"What?" he says checking both arms.

"That red thing. Over there." I point it out for him.

"This? Oh, I guess an insect bit me. It's okay, it probably needed me. You know how insects are."

"Mmm, no, I don't."

"Come on, isn't your dad the Lord of the Insects?" he jokes, "See, Thomas, insects are the most independent beings in the world. They survive on their own. But sometimes, insects need something else. Sometimes they need to stop figuring things out on their own. They need help."

"And they bite humans?"

"Correction, they suck wisdom from humans."

"You are fucking crazy, Billy."

"Aren't we all? In this place we are all a

combination of crazy humans, bad-ass insects, and amazing princesses."

Fucking Billy Jean. Fucking princess.

"Come on, I'm *starving*," he says.

"I'll meet you there," I say.

Billy Jean leaves. I walk back to the pool. I take a long look at it. I take a long look at everything around it.

I think of Sean. No, Sean wasn't there. Sean is nowhere to be found. Sean will only be here, in my heart.

* * *

I tell Norma about my swimming experience the next day. I tell her I wasn't trying to kill myself or anything. I tell her I was actually just swimming.

"I feel better now. I'm sad and shit but I feel stronger. I feel ready. I think it's time."

"Time for what?" she asks.

"Time to go. Time to leave this place."

"Are you ready for your parents?"

"I don't think I will ever be ready for them, but, oh well," I confess.

"So what will you do?"

"I was thinking of spending some time with my brother, in Montreal. Take it slowly and then . . . "

"And then?"

"We'll see."

"Sounds like a plan. I say we talk to Dr. Stevens and see what he thinks. Okay? But I bet pretty soon we will be able to call your dad and let him know that you're ready."

"Excellent."

* * *

I'm leaving the teen mental clinic after being here almost three months. Billy Jean and I exchange addresses, phone numbers, emails, hugs and kisses. I have found a friend for life.

I say goodbye to my room and my life in this

place. I say goodbye to everyone: the people in group therapy, the nurses, and the whole staff. I thank Norma and Dr. Stevens.

My parents pick me up. Yes, Mom came along. She doesn't know what to say when she sees me. I don't know what to tell her, either. Things cannot change that much in three months, but for the first time I feel almost happy to see her and that's new.

"You hungry?" she asks, and, as always, she doesn't give me a chance to reply. "Of course, you are. Let's get something good for the kid, honey."

Dad smiles and says, "Okay. What do you feel like Edna?"

"Whatever you want," she says.

"How about steak?"

"Steak sounds good," I say.

"Steak? No, let's get chicken," Mom states.

I can't say I missed their arguments or that I missed them, but their disagreement already makes me feel at home.

"Chicken sounds good," I say.

"Chicken it is," Dad agrees.

"Dad?"

"Yes?"

"Can you teach me about insects?"

"What do you mean?" he asks intrigued. Mom turns to look at me. She too is intrigued by my words.

"Talk to me about insects. Tell me all you know."

"Well, your dad knows *a lot* about insects," Mom says, "So you need to be more specific."

"I wanna learn everything."

"Really? Why?"

"Just because."

"You know? Insects are the most intelligent beings in this world," Dad says. "I don't know why people use the word *insect* as an insult, it is actually a compliment."

I'm looking forward to going home. I know there will be ups and downs. I know Mom and I will still yell at each other. I know Dad will spend lots of time with his insect books, but now I will be there, right next to him. Learning. I'm ready now. I want to see the tall green pines outside the clinic. I want to see what life is about beyond these gates.